Mana B

Amulet of Heroes

Book 1

By Mark Tillotson

Book also by Mark Tillotson

Short Stories
The Shadow and the Fox
Fates of the Wind
Broken

First published in Great Britain in 2021
Copyright © 2021 Mark Tillotson
All rights reserved.
ISBN: 9798524354778

Mana Borne Short stories collection, novels, and appendix by
Mark Tillotson

Dedications

to my amazing partner and best friend Alice. You have encouraged me to pursue my dreams and helped push me to finally write this story.

To my parents and family for always supporting me.

Prologue

If any of those shall find this book, let it be known the wonders of the ancient world. From the farthest reaches of the rolling southern deserts and plains, to the northern snow wastes, the people of this world have lived in peace for centuries but that was never the case.
Nearly a thousand years ago, darkness threatened to destroy the world and enslave its people. This turbulent time came to be known by the survivors as 'The Dawning'.

The ancient city of Cyrilla once housed the greatest and first civilisations of man. This sprawling city of the north spanned for miles, dotted with ornate spires of stone and gold. Its people were once seen as the pinnacle of wisdom throughout the known world, with many able to use Mana. This mysterious force known as Mana, had the power to manipulate the world itself for the few that could use it. For as long as history has been recorded, some people have been able to use Mana with such skill, twisting it and moulding, some for knowledge and understanding while others for their own ill-gotten gains. In Cyrilla, its people were trained to use it responsibly.

Every once in a while, someone would be born that showed a natural talent more than others. As the many years passed in peace one such sorcerer, Cirdire, became quite gifted in its use and understanding. Even as a child he trained day and night with the masters, ever seeking further understanding of Mana and its origins. As he grew older and more experienced, his thirst for more knowledge often drove him to question his teachers and the rules imposed by Cyrilla's ruling council. One thing this adventurous sorcerer did not expect was a being to speak to him from the void, a plane of existence from where Mana originates. The voice began offering him a chance to learn everything he ever wanted in exchange, he would help it enter the world of men.

Failing to heed the words of his mentors, Cirdire left Cyrilla behind and headed to Telloma, the tallest mountain in Terrerth. For months he spent communing with the voice, learning the incantations to open a rift between worlds. The masters of Cyrilla in turn began to sense an impending darkness, sending mages out to try and search for Cirdire to stop him, but they were too late. The rift between the worlds caused an earthquake devastating the land and darkened the skies over Telloma. Cities, towns, and villages shook leagues away from the mountain, even ships on the oceans were met with huge tsunami's coming from the shores. Emerging from the rift was a being in the form of a young woman. Her skin as pale as the snow and adorned in a ripped dress and blindfolded, she revealed her name to the young sorcerer. Shassa the voice of the Abyss.

Promising to give the sorcerer everything, she ensnared the young Cirdire with her beauty. Whilst powerful, she was still weakened in this new realm, as she slowly began to bend him to her will, she tore out his soul and corrupted his body until only a withered husk remained. This withered and tormented being was dubbed Nightshade. Shassa bound him to her and forced him to lead her legions of demonic beings and the Aptrogon. The Aptrogon, a foul and unholy undead, decayed soldier risen through necromancy and driven by their new masters.

Across the land they slowly marched, its purpose to enslave all beings.

Foreseeing their destruction, Cyrilla raised an army of warriors both Manaborne and Non-magic users, they called themselves the Lightbringers. This alliance swept south to meet the scourge of Shassa. The bloody war raged for years, battles covered the land as the forces of Light and dark fought for dominion of the world. It was during the battle of Fellanre river that two soldiers started to emerge as legendary warriors. Arturus, a Mana-wielding sorcerer and his twin sister Bellatris rose through the ranks. Backed by their armies, Arturus used his powers and forces to sweep the western lands while Bellatris and her ruthless warriors purged the east.

In the closing days of the war, the final battle was decided in the expansive Telloma forest. There, the Lightbringers fought the forces of Shassa amongst the densely packed trees. Hour after hour sorcerers pushed back the Aptrogon as the warriors clashed swords, Demons and sorcerers duelled, the roots and ground were stained with blood. Between the roots snaked a crimson river of blood as it flowed and pooled into bogs. Soldiers and demons alike struggled to trudge through the thick swamps. Arturus had wielded unsuppressed Mana as group after group of undead were obliterated, finally meeting up with Bellatris at the maw of Telloma.

Both warriors, exhausted from the battle, navigated the caverns until finally they reached the heart of the mountain. The cavern stretched as far as the eye could see, engulfed in shadows. In the middle, a single stone plinth held the entrance to the rift, its maw warping as blue and purple light illuminated the area around it. As they cautiously moved closer to the rift, the darkness began to change. Rushing around them, it lashed and whipped at the twins until finally Nightshade stood before them. Bellatris and Arturus had barely recognised the demonic being that had once been their friend, it's skin grey and cracked like ash and purple eyes glowing from the darkness.

The three champions battled for hours with such ferocity the likes that no living man or woman had ever seen. Nearing the climax of the battle Shassa herself emerged from the rift. Shassa's form of a young woman transformed into an ungodly and monstrous banshee. Knowing they could not battle such a foe, Arturus channelled his last remaining Mana unleashing a force that rendered Nightshade to his knees. With Nightshade defeated, Shassa was forced back into the Abyss and the rift sealed. With all his strength drained, the remaining Lightbringers joined together to seal Nightshade into a Stone tomb, never to be released again. The entrance to the mountain was closed and hidden.

With the war finally at an end the dawn of a new age was upon them. Fighting for many years, experiencing and enduring hardships no one from Cyrilla could ever understand, the twins knew they could never return home. The two discussed for days what should be done, each had their differences. Arturus wanted people to learn from the past and continue to study Mana in a more supervised way. Bellatris however had grown to despise Mana and wished the world to never allow such a war to happen again through intimidation and force. Both fought each other until finally they realised, they would never agree. The siblings finally both went their separate ways.

For decades Arturus had moved south and founded Artheria, named by his army in honour of him. Artheria soon became the beacon of knowledge and learning. Its streets built of bright sandstone; it's academy's towers could be seen for miles around. Bellatris however moved east towards the lands she had liberated during the war. Laying on the banks of the Doomerne river, she founded the fortress city of Beltoria. Ring wall after ring wall, mighty iron gates and at its centre the Lord's tower. This imposing city dominates the lands of the north and rules without question.

A Day Like Any Other
Chapter 1

With a soft close of the book, it was over. Master Pret sat and smiled as all the children of the town sat with mouths open in awe of the story. He enjoyed teaching the children of the past, often remarking to them as well as the villagers of Rheia, on the importance of knowing never to repeat the mistakes. This was something that he had some experience from his youth. Amongst the children, one in particular stood out to him as always. Kyle keenly listened to every word of the old tomes that his teacher kept. Fascinated by the heroes and villains of the past, Kyle fantasized about his own adventures. Sat amongst a couple other children he was an average teen boy from his village. There was nothing special about his brunette hair or the slightly tattered clothes he dressed in. Even his size was normal for a teenager. For all intents and purposes, he was an ordinary boy.

The group sat underneath a large Oak tree in the centre of a small stone courtyard, the buildings that surrounded them were as natural as the stone they were carved into. Set into the cliff faces the monks had spent centuries carving and decorating every column, every doorway in such beauty. For years Kyle frequently looked at the depictions of the bygone eras, but his favourite was the mural of the battle of Fellanre.

"That my students, I feel is enough today." Master Pret croaked; his voice was of a man who spent a lifetime talking.

"Why wouldn't they stick together? Or go home?" One of the boys asked. Pret smiled as he looked around until he found a couple twigs on the ground. Holding them out,

"Do you see these twigs? If I was to break them." Pret snapped them gently in-between his hands, "Can they ever be the same again?"

The children muttered amongst themselves as Kyle watched from the back. He always enjoyed Master Pret's teachings, riddles that were so hard until the answer laid in front so clearly. As he scanned the group watching them deliberate on the simple answer, his eyes was drawn to a girl sitting next to another. Smiling as she talked to the other girl, Kyle held his gaze. A natural beauty of long auburn hair, sweet emerald eyes and such feminine features, Kyle thought she was as beautiful as a spring morning. For years he and Lucia had come to the monastery to learn, until they had become top students.

"Anybody?" Pret sat patiently.

"No."

"Exactly. No one who ever goes into war or even a battle ever can be the same again."

Kyle sat quietly mulling over the notion while the rest of the group started to talk to each other.

"Do you think there will ever be another war?" A little boy asked. Kyle and the rest of the children snapped a look to Master Pret, waiting on bated breath for his response. In his usual way, Pret smiled and leaned forward, "We have lived in peace for a thousand years, so, no I am quite certain we will be fine."

The rest of the cold morning slowly gave way to the warm midday sun as the children returned to the boats they had so eagerly arrived on. Spending the remainder of his morning under the familiar Oak tree, Kyle read through one of the books in peace. He had explored every inch of the island but nowhere had felt as comfortable as being sat under this tree. Page by page he threw himself into the adventure, every monster he slew every battle he fought excited his imagination. Master Pret made his way through the courtyard to see Kyle sat alone under the tree, content in his imagination. Pret slowly made his way over towards him. His old age had caught up years ago, reducing his posture to a stooped elder.

"Ah the tale of the Dwarves I see."

Kyle looked up at the sight of a looming shadow. "Yes sir, I hope you don't mind me taking it from the library?" Kyle said anxiously.

"Not at all," said Pret with a smile, "I find myself regularly falling into stories of the past." Kyle saw a gleam in Pret's eye. 'A long past adventurer' he thought. Pret never spoke about his past, only the history of others. Almost everyone from the village thought the monks lived here all their lives, never venturing into the world but somehow, they knew all the stories.

"Which is your favourite Master Pret?" Kyle said inquisitively. Pret mulled it over for a moment trying to recall a distant memory.

"I would have to say the tale of Nightshade."

Kyle was stunned by the answer. Nearly everyone knew the tale of Nightshade, how he fell to darkness and started the Dawning war. Kyle was so surprised by the answer, it began to creep across his face.

"You disapprove?"

Kyle began to stutter "No sir, I'm just surprised."

"And why is that?" Pret questioned "I believe it has one of the most important messages of all."

Out of the corner of his eye, Kyle saw a man waving towards him. Even from this distance he could make out the outline of his father, Tomen. A rather large man both in height and shoulders, his midsection slowly filling out.

"Kyle it's time to go, the tide is going out."

Without a word Kyle hopped to his feet and started walking towards his father, Master Pret walking beside him.

"Master, Nightshade was an evil demon who traded his soul for power." Pret continued to walk with a smile upon his face.

"Yes, he did and that itself should mean something." They reached the entrance to the monastery, beyond the entrance was a simple beach where the boats docked and across the narrow water laid the small village of Rheia. Pret turned to Kyle and puts his hand out Kyle's shoulder. "Knowledge is a dangerous thing, to seek it out is wise but be careful not to wish for things, sometimes they may come true. Nightshade paid the price for his vanity; we should all be careful not to do the same." Kyle didn't understand the meaning of it all, but he trusted Master Pret's words. As he began to head towards the boats, Kyle suddenly stopped and held out the book. "Keep it, enjoy the adventures until next time."

"Thank you, I'll see you in a couple of days." Kyle quickly turned and ran down the path to the boats. Pret watched as they slowly pushed away from shore. From where he stood the clouds began to darker as a storm slowly moved in from the sea however, this wasn't the only darkness he could feel approaching.

The journey across the narrow water was as uneventful as ever. The cool sea breeze splashed against their faces as the bow of the boat crashed into the waves. Kyle sat in the corner hoping to read a couple more pages, but his mind was still drifting back to the stories of the morning.

"Kyle, I need your help." Tomen called out. Kyle put his book down and looked to his father. "Grab the rudder while I sort of the Jib line." Kyle staggered to his feet as the boat rocked. For years he'd sailed with his father on the boats but still he struggled to find his feet, Tomen regularly compared him to a new-born lamb. Clambering towards the stern Kyle grabbed a hold of the rudder and kept it tight.

"This storm is quite strong." Kyle pointed out as Tomen effortlessly walked to the bow. "Will we be ok?"

"We'll be fine, just a bit strange for this time of year." Tomen had been a fisherman most of his life, sailing in all kinds of weather from calm to raging seas, yet somehow, he seemed uneasy about this one.

"Why is it strange?" Kyle asked. Tomen remained quiet as he sorted out the rigging.

"It's nothing, let's get home to the girls. Your mother will be worried."

After an hour of sailing and finally anchoring the boats onto the beach, Kyle and the others made the short journey back to their village. Rheia was a small village of mostly farmers, a bakery, a tavern, and a small hall but this quaint community had been around as long as the monastery. Kyle had never had any trouble finding other children to play with, in a community as small as theirs, everyone was familiar with everyone. Sometimes that was not always a good thing, his mother Alexia frequently spoke of the grape vine in Rheia, secrets within the village were seldom. From a distance they could make out the sight of his sister Rose. A small, bright young girl began to shout out

"Mummy, mummy they're back!" Rose began to run towards them both, her little legs scrambling to keep her upright. Bounding towards them Rose ran into the arms of her father, overjoyed to see him again.

"My dear Rosey, how is my little girl?" Tomen exclaimed. The look of a father lovingly holding his daughter was a priceless sight for a family that didn't have much more than each other. Standing by the house, a gorgeous blonde woman stood waiting patiently for her family to return. His mother Alexia was considered the most beautiful in the village. Even as a young woman, many men called upon her, but it was Tomen, an adventuring young man, that captured her eye and eventually her heart. Tomen, Kyle and Rose finally reached Alexia and embraced together.

The Coming Storm
Chapter 2

The storm continued to roll towards the shore, its harsh winds whipping the sea into a frenzy as it battered the shoreline heaving to and fro. The sky filled with angry clouds, covering every inch that not even the brightest star could pierce it.

Huddled against the wooden wall of his house, Kyle could see the trees bash together in the roaring wind, the sound of the sea and leaves merged together. Lit only by candlelight, Kyle continued to read his book, the light flickering in the wind as it seeped between the boards of the walls. On the page, a picture depicting the final battle of the Dwarves, the siege of Naz-Ard. He glided his fingers over pencil drawings of the buildings and rock. Kyle was fascinated by the Dwarves, an ancient race of strong warriors and craftsmen. He thought many times that it was a shame he and so many others would never get to see them. Their extinction had long since passed from legend and then into myth.

"Kyle, supper time." Alexia spoke softly. Kyle looked up to the smiling face of his mother and nodded. "What are you reading now?" she asked.

"It's about Dwarves and the battle of Naz-Ard" He replied. His excitement about the topic showed through his face.

"You're brave reading such stories before bed."

"Not really, I just wish they were still around. I'd have loved to have seen them." Kyle closed his book and placed it down on his bed.

"Well dear time to eat, come on." Alexia said as she turned to walk back into the living area. A speck of colour caught his eye from between the crack of his wall. He Looked out to see a small glimmer of a fire way up into the hillside amongst the trees, like a fleck of orange on a black canvas.

Beyond the borders of the village and amongst the treeline a small fire burned desperately against the wind and rain. A small group huddled together trying badly to stay warm, but one man stood defiantly against the storm. Keela had spent many nights in the wilderness, battling the elements, fighting to survive, to him this was no different from any other night but tonight it was all going to change. Looking out over sea towards the monastery on the island, small flickers of light could be seen battling against the wind and rain. Keela stroked a scar on the back of his left hand, it was a deep scar running from his knuckles all the way up to his elbow, a stark reminder of his time in the wild.

"Sir?" a voice came from behind him. Keela looked over his shoulder to see Ariel standing hooded and cloaked. Her pale white skin was the only colour seen against the night that surrounded them. "What are we doing here?" Ariel questioned. To Keela she was a faithful second, but he found she lacked sight of the larger plans. Turning around slowly his size was made apparent by the light of the fire. An intimidating sight, he wore a black hooded cloak himself, one hand covered in metal gauntlet on his right side, a sword strapped to his waist. He slowly walked past her towards the fire.

"Waiting." Keela said ominously. Raising his hand over the fire, the flames began to burn brighter and taller as if dancing like a puppet to its master.

"Waiting for what Master? If the relic is over there we should go now and take it!" Ariel's voice grew with excitement at the prospect of a fight. Too many cold nights in the wild had started to chill her appetite for violence.

"No." Keela replied. "I sense the presence of a relic in that monastery. We *will* attack tomorrow night." His voice resonated through everyone as he stared at Ariel. His stare cut deep into the soul of Ariel until she bowed her head submissively.

The group began to mutter to each other as the wind whipped up again.

Turning again Keela walked away from the fire into the darkness beyond the light of the fire. After a couple feet into the blackness, he suddenly stopped to the sound of a voice.

"Keela, my child." It whispered. Keela felt the voice grow louder in his mind, his eyes starting to glow blue.

"Yes Master." Keela replied, all his authority drained from him as a vision appeared in front. A faceless and formless shade moved around him, the darkness consuming all the light behind it as if absorbing it.

"Have you found the key?" the voice hissed, echoing inside his head. Keela watched as it floated around him.

"Yes Master, it is inside a temple nearby. I will find it and then we will be one step closer my lord."

"This temple is a lie, they hide the true power of this world. Darkness can never be destroyed. They *must* be punished." The voice whispered, its malice lingered on every word.

"I will make them tell us its location. The light cannot stand against the coming darkness."

"And when you are done my child. When their bodies are beaten, and their spirits are broken." The shade came to a stop in front of Keela's face. "Burn them!" the shade shrieked as it charged into Keela's body. He shuddered and shook as the apparition finally disappeared leaving him alone in the black forest. He had stood against cold nights and long storms, but he had felt a chill as cold as the shade when it revealed itself. A moment went by as warmth returned with all his strength. With a renewed vigour Keela returned to his camp and sat down beside the fire. "Tomorrow we begin our journey." Keela eyed each one of his disciples. Each responded with a nod or smile. "Long live the lord of Darkness".

More than Meets the Eye
Chapter 3

The next day as the winds and rain had finally passed, Kyle and his father set sail in the early morning sun, it's warm golden light creeping up from the horizon like a beacon. Seagulls cycled above the shore as they called out to one another eagerly eying up the fishermen as they dragged their haul ashore. Dozens of the town residents relied on the sea for their food but also their livelihood. For years Kyle had helped his father fish the sea and still he struggled with the early morning starts. Tomen often jokingly remarked about his teenage years as well. Today was like any other day as the sea gently rocked the boat as they went about their duties.

"Kyle check the nets?" Tomen ordered. Kyle did as he was told as he hoisted the nets up. As he reached the end of the netting it still remained empty, 'Three hours and still nothing.' Tomen thought.

"This is strange indeed, usually there is at least half a boatful by now. We'll sail east more out into the sea. We should find some there."

Kyle hoped they would soon. On days like this his mind always wandered thinking about all the adventures he could be having rather than sitting on a boat. None of the heroes in his books sat on a boat, they wandered the lands looking for beasts to slay and maidens to save.

Another hour went by as he waited for the fish to come, Kyle looked out over the water thinking of the distant lands beyond, from the Forests of Laxos to the great glass plains or the deserts.

"How long has it been now?" Kyle asked. Tomen knew they had been out a while, even he started to question whether to keep going. Looking up at the sun which now sat high above them, "It's past midday now, we should start thinking about heading back.".

In the very faint distance Kyle could make out a ship on the horizon. Even from across the expanse he could see the tall masts standing tall on its deck and its sails catching the wind.

"What ship is that father?" Kyle asked as he pointed to it. Tomen strained his eyes in the sun to see it, but he could see the tall doubled masted ship.

"It's a trading galley from Tyrus."

"Have you ever been there? I mean to places beyond the sea?" The excitement of asking his father about his stories fascinated him.

"Aye I have. A couple of times, when I once worked on a galley like that, it's a beautiful place. The streets go on from miles and miles, markets that are bigger than Rheia and people from all corners of the world. I even met a man from Eshret Desert, such a foreign and strange place." Tomen retorted. Kyle couldn't help but smile at the wonders his father had seen and one day he might be able to look upon. Kyle tried asking about his father's adventures and sometimes he would tell a few tales, but most of the time he kept his past secret. He had only seen the world through books but many never ventured across the waters to distant lands. Kyle always savoured the chance to journey to the monastery and its library. Although it was small, every now and then he would find a book that came from one of those lands. He had recently read a book that described beasts from the desert, Desert worms that were larger than horses and lived under the sand, multi-coloured birds where a single feather was worth more than people's houses. With a look of disappointment at their catch Tomen threw down his hat. "Pull the nets in son, we should head back. I don't think we'll find much more now."

A few unremarkable hours passed by as they sailed west back home, the sun guiding them. Tomen sat quietly at the stern of the ship, his eye on the horizon and hand on the rudder. Kyle lay slumped against the hull, his head hanging over the side. The cool sea spray felt nice against his skin as he had his hand in the water breaking through the waves, his mind wandering again. The minutes passed by but as he stared out over the water he felt a strange sensation in his head, as if someone had placed their hand on his head. Kyle turned around expecting to see his father smiling down at him, instead he saw nothing, just Tomen at the rear of the boat. He turned his attention back to the water and went back to his imagination. After a few moments the sensation returned except this time he heard something. He concentrated on the sound as it grew clearer. The low hum echoed as it turned into the whisper of a voice, as if it was being carried on the sea winds, the words still too faint to hear.
"Father, can you hear that?" Kyle turned to Tomen.
"Here what?"
"A voice. I hear a voice out there." Tomen looked out to sea in every direction, his eyes like a hawk as it scoured every way.
"I don't hear or see anything." Tomen smiled at him, "I'm sure it's just your imagination running wild again." Kyle hated it when they said it's his imagination, blaming the books he constantly read. He turned back to look out for himself again still, he saw no one in the water. The voice called out to Kyle again for an instant.

"Kyle."

The sensation in his head clouded his thoughts for a moment. As he looked at the breaking water against his hand, the water began to move around it differently. In instinct Kyle raised his hand from the water, as he did the water started to pull with him. 'What is going on?' Kyle thought as he continued to pull his hand until it finally left the sea. Water leaped out of the sea and began to flow around his hand and fingertips. The sensation in his head dulled and finally disappeared entirely. As it vanished the water around his hand fell back into the sea leaving only an astonished boy.

Expecting to hear amazement from his father, Kyle turned to look. Staring back at him with an unsurprised expression on his face, Tomen smirked.

"I was beginning to wonder if your gift was going to emerge." A thousand thoughts ran through his mind 'How did he know? Why didn't he say anything?"

"What happened?" Kyle asked moving away from the edge of the boat.

"You focused Mana for the first-time son and a good first attempt as well. The first time I did it I nearly pulled the branches from a tree. I was starting to wonder if you had the ability at all." Still in shock, Kyle sat quietly as he tried to comprehend the last few minutes. For many years he read all the stories and tales of heroes and their adventures, never in his wildest dreams did he think he might *actually be* like one of them.

Finally plucking the courage to ask, Kyle turned to Tomen "How did you know?" Tomen kept his focus on the now growing shoreline. Along the beach stood his fellow fishermen as they moored and tied down their boats for the night.

"There are a great many things Master Pret has not told you." Tomen stood up as he rained in his sail. "But very soon you'll know that our family has a great many secrets of our own."

A History Uncovered
Chapter 4

Kyle and his father spent the next few hours dragging the boat ashore and made their way back to the house. The journey was long and silent as Kyle tried to stir up the courage to ask his father what exactly had happened. Rhea and its townspeople had settled down for the evening as the last of the shop owners closed their doors. The sun once again dipping behind the horizon painting the clouds in a sea of orange and red hues. At the centre of the village the town hall was still open, light and laughter spilt out from the door as the people drank and feasted. Kyle sometimes enjoyed going there when the town had an event because it gave him a chance to listen to the adults tell stories or play with the other kids, but he hated the hoppy smell of the ale. His father offered him some on his fifteenth birthday, but all he could do was spit it out in disgust. Everyone laughed in his reaction but he knew it was all in good fun.

Kyle and Tomen continued along the street towards their house as the sounds of the town faded into silence. Kyle had imagined about having his own powers, to feel the Mana flow through him and what he might do with it. He pictured himself as a knight, using it to protect the innocent from bandits. Finally, his mind didn't drift to the past, instead it focused on the future.

"Father, what did you mean about our family?" He said looking at Tomen who smiled back at him. They continued to walk in silence until they reached home. Taking a few steps up until Tomen placed his tools down on the small porch of their home and sat on his bench by the door. It creaked loudly as he finally came to rest with his back lent against the wall.

"What I'm about to tell you is the real history of our family, passed down from my father and his fathers before him." Tomen gestured his hand for Kyle to sit down opposite him.

"There is a reason why only a few of us get to go to the monastery and deal with the monks. This town was founded centuries ago by our ancestors and the Lightbringers from the Dawning War. Some of the Lightbringers were convinced that they needed to remove themselves from the world in the hope they could come to terms with the horrors they had witnessed. Those Lightbringers were the ones that founded the monastery. The soldiers from that army vowed to protect the Mana users as they went into seclusion, in return the monks would trade, teach and guide us." Kyle's eyes widened as the truth about his home emerged.

"If we're the descendants of the soldiers? How do we have powers?" Kyle asked.

"Don't mistake them as powers, we don't own Mana, it's not ours." Tomen looked into his sack and lifted out a fisherman's thread holding open in his palm. "Mana works through us, it exists beyond this world, beyond the stars but at the same time, it is all these things." Without moving the thread, it began to levitate in his hand. Kyle's eyes fixed on the rotating tool until without any effort it split into two strands. Kyle jumped back at the snap. Still hovering above his father's hand, the fragments floated about like dust in the wind. Kyle slowly moved forward staring wondrously at the pieces. Now with his face only a few inches from the pieces Kyle reached out to touch them. Tomen smiled as his focus returned back on the thread. Kyle pulled back his hand. "It has no malice or love,

it just… is." The fragments slowly moved back together, and the fractures receded until it became whole again.
"How did you do that? Can I fix things like you?" Kyle asked reaching out for the tool and began to play with the thread in his hands, each finger tracing where the fractures used to be. Hearing footsteps coming from inside, they both turned to see Alexia learning against the door frame.
"Mother, it happened! I did it!" Standing up he held out the thread to her, focusing as hard as he could on the tool, but nothing happened.
"He managed to manipulate the water whilst we were out today." Tomen remarked as he watched Kyle try harder to move the object. Alexia leaned over and placed her hand on his shoulder.
"It will come in time my dear, I'm sure Idella's blessing will show you your way."
Whenever Kyle was frustrated, Alexia always managed to calm him with her touch. Some people called it the blessing on the mother goddess, but to him it was always just his mother.
"When will I know what I can do?" Kyle looked away disheartened. The sun had finally started to creep below the treetops turning the sky into a mixture of purples and oranges.
"Soon, do not worry." She smiled. Kyle looked at his father.
"What about Rose and Alistair? Will they get powers?"
They both looked at each other, as if they knew this question was going to be asked, a glimpse into their own childhood when they discovered their abilities for the first time.
"They will in time, when their time is right." Tomen said standing up, his tired body struggling. "I think this is

enough for now, it's a lot to take in and it's been a long day." Tomen made his way into the house leaving Kyle to comprehend his new heritage. Unable to look at his mother, Kyle slumped down onto the step of the porch and looked at his hands. Thinking back to the water, the only thing that he could remember was the voice flowing on the wind, the sensations across his body.

"Your father is proud of you, although he may not always say it." Alexia sat down next to him and nudged him.

"You know I was only a little younger than you when I first realised what I could do. It terrified me so much I thought it was a nightmare." Kyle watched carefully as she raised her hand towards a group of saplings in the grass. Within a matter of seconds, the saplings grew and flowered into beautiful white snowdrops. Speechless and in awe, Kyle had heard of the abilities of mages in the past but never had he thought watching it happen could be as amazing. Master Pret never showed his powers in the presence of anyone of the villagers and when Kyle had asked once why he replied with a stern look.

Out of the Shadows
Chapter 5

A stillness settled over the waters as if the evening cool breeze was stopped, the only noise was the sound of the boat's bow breaking on the water. The starlight above shone but didn't reflect on the water around them as if it had been swallowed up. Stood silently, Keela focused his attention on the rising stone walls of the monastery. The moonlight shining down on them, the walls towered over the island cliff face with authority, every natural crack and crevice like veins on the stone.

For the next few minutes the boat slowly paddled towards the northern side of the island until finally the boat ramped up onto the shoreline. One by one Keela and the rest swiftly exited the boat and made their way up the hillside. They moved with such grace and speed it was as if a shadow itself moved. Every step Keela took, the feeling of hate grew in him from somewhere, the unbridled malice forcing him to march quicker. Finally, they reached the unguarded gates of the monastery. They stood silently, the only light from the torches that adorned the entrance and quad. Keela scanned the tunnel, his viper like eyes slow but determined. The feeling was palpable to Keela as he took in the moment, years spent looking and now it was within his grasp.

"Begin." Keela ordered as he turned to Ariel. Without any sign of emotion, she pulled a mask up to her eyes and unsheathed her dagger. The handle was carved into the shape of a dragon and its blade curved and jagged like a tooth. On the blade itself engravings of symbols ran up the centre to the hilt.

Keela remembered the day he gave her the knife, much like this night, she proved her love for him by killing her parents with it. Like himself she knew that power always came with consequences and for her it would be no different. The blade took the souls from its victims and of the wielder. Ariel both loved and hated the knife, but her devotion to Keela proved more powerful.

Taking her first steps into the monastery, she made no sound. Footstep after footstep she moved like a feline along the walls. As she passed the torches each one faded and extinguished until finally Ariel faded into the darkness of the building. One by one each of Keela's followers entered and spread out across the temple. Inside the hate had finally revealed itself as the formless being appeared beside him.

"It is here, I feel it." Its whisper echoed inside his mind. "Bring me the icon." A shape on the wall caught Keela's attention. Turning towards it, he raised his hand towards the burnt-out torches igniting them into life in an instant. Etched into the wall, an epitaph of magnificent size, stretching twenty metres wide and five metres high it told the story of the Dawning War. On the far left, the Lightbringers march towards the centre led by Arturus and his sister Bellatris. On the right, the forces of Shassa led by Nightshade. At the centre of the carving the portal to Shassa at the abyss. In the centre a small seven-pointed symbol was carved.

"Soon she will arrive, and all will burn." Keela was still engrossed by the wall and remained silent. Feelings of power began to rise in him, an ancient feeling that had long been forgotten. The formless being faded away into the shadows as a monk turned the corner instantly freezing. Without any concern Keela turned to look at the frightened monk, his scarred face staring back at him.

"Master!" the monk shouted, turning to run away.

Standing in front of the monk silent and still, Ariel slipped the dagger into his chest. Pain and fear spread across his face as his life began to drain away from him. Ariel's eyes turned black as if all the light in the world could not escape, her skin began to glow as the youth came back to her. Only a few moments passed until a lifeless husk fell to the floor, withered and dry. Ariel took a deep breath in as the last of the monk's lifeforce filled her up. She looked down at the knife in her hand, the blood still stained on the blade.

Inside his private chamber, Pret knelt in meditation. Preferring simple decoration, his room only adored with a bed, table, chair and mat. Each night Pret reflected on his craft, always feeling the power within the monastery, tonight however something was dire. Hovering above his body, his medallion flowed around him, each piece orbiting a small emerald orb at the centre.

The sound of rising voices and bells broke his focus as the medallion snapped back together. As he rose to his feet the door to his chamber burst open. Before him two men stood dressed in black, hooded and cloaked. The two charged forward and in instinct Pret raised his hand unleashing a gust of furious wind hitting the men suddenly launching them back into the wall. Before he could move the feeling of cold steel laid across his throat. Ariel appeared from behind as if she had melted through the wall.

"Where is it?" Ariel asked, pressing the blade harder against his skin.

"Do what you came to do, I shall not tell you assassin."
Pret pushed his throat against the blade further until a
speck of blood appeared. "There is nothing you or that
foul blade can do to make me tell you otherwise."
"No?" A sound of enjoyment in her tone. "I can't but, my
Master *will*." A sharp blow to the back of Pret's head
knocks him to the floor.

Snaps and cracks rang out in Pret's ears as he slowly
roused from his assault. The smell of burning wood, books
and flesh filled his nose, overwhelming his senses until his
eyes finally opened. The calm dark night had given way to
the lashing colours of fire. Laying on the floor in the
courtyard the buildings around him were alight and
crumbling under the inferno. A lifetime of devotion and
countless generations of history gone, were more painful
than anything he thought possible. As his eyes came into
focus so did the shadowy spectres that surrounded him.
To his right, two monks, knives to their throats and in front
of him standing tall, Keela. Still facing the wall, the light
from the burning buildings illuminated the entire wall.
"There is nothing here that is worth taking assassin." Pret
croaked. "Take what little treasure we have and go."
"Assassins?" Keela turned to face Pret, the look of malice
in his eyes burning as brightly as the flames around them.
"You small minded old fool. If we were assassins, you
would not be speaking." Keela came to stand directly in
front of Pret. Raising his head to look up at the imposing
figure, Pret noticed the light around Keela seemed to be
absorbed leaving him in near entire blackness. There was
an old feeling stirring in the back of his mind, as if he'd felt
this powerful darkness before.
"Tell me where it is, and I'll spare you and your...
followers." Keela demanded pointing to the monks. Pret

looked to his brother and sister as they stared back. Each one knowing what is about to happen.

"I will not."

"So be it." Keela moved towards the woman who tried to hold back her fear. Looming over her like death itself, Keela raised his hand and forced it onto her chest. The fires gave way to a blood curdling shriek as Keela ripped her soul from her body. Her scream faded into an echo as the last ounce of life was stripped from her body. In Keela's grasp the soul of the terrified woman silently screaming out. Everyone looked on as Keela crushed against the spectre's throat until finally the soul shattered and faded into nothing. A moment of ecstasy rolled over his face as Keela turned back to Pret. It finally hit him. He had met this person decades ago in his youth whilst investigating a mysterious dig site. Pret had only just managed thwart Keela's plan and left him with a noticeable scar on his arm.

"I cannot give you what you ask." Pret pleaded.

"I am not asking anymore. Give me the Icon!"

Keela pointed towards the next monk. As if she was the wind, Ariel moves towards the monk. Defiant like his master, Pret looks back to his brother one last time.

"Idella bless you brother." In a slow-motion Ariel stabbed the dagger into the man's back as the life began to drain from his body. Pret watched on helplessly as the life surged through her body as it stripped away from his fellow monk.

"For you Master Pret, it will not be so quick." Keela Turned to look back at Pret and knelt eye to eye. Pret saw the fires around them burning in Keela's eyes but beyond that, some hidden evil watched. Placing a hand on Master Pret's chest, the pain immediately intensified forcing a scream of pain out.

The Rising Fire
Chapter 6

For hours Kyle slept peacefully under the watchful eye of
his mother and father. Alexia looked on with pride at her
Kyle, Tomen however was troubled by something. Gently
resting her hand on his knee, "There is nothing to worry
about. We knew this day would come."
Tomen's gaze lingered for a moment before being drawn
to his wife. For as long as he knew her, she had the ability
to lift any doubt in his mind, 'a gift like no other' he
thought. On this night though, the worry in his mind was
stronger than usual. Glancing back over to Kyle who was
sleeping soundly "He is too young to know."
"He's spent so much time with his head in those books,
they've filled his head with fantasy. I fear the world will
crush him."
Alexia leaned over to lift a large iron stoker to the fire.
Calmly she began to shuffle the wood and charcoal
around. Each shift produced a plume of beautiful embers
that floated and drifted into the sky before fading into the
night.
"Tomen look at these embers." Tomen complied and
looked at the floating fireflies in front of him. "Each one of
these embers are like children, birthed from the fire and
destined to float away. Some will land and start their own
fires which will create their own embers, others will fade
away." Tomen looked at Alexia who watched in awe at the
rising embers. For a young beautiful woman, she was wise.
Some people in the village had accused her of being a
witch because of her gifts. Each time they spoke out he
would rush to defend her, fist raised, and each time Alexia
would speak softly to them. After only a short time both

parties would calm as if all the anger was stripped away from them.

"It is the fate of all children to leave their parents and explore." She turned to look at Tomen. "All you have to do is best to prepare them for the world ahead." For a brief moment, time felt as if it slowed to a halt as they stared into each other's eyes. As the two moved in for a kiss, the moment was broken by a scream from outside. The children stirred as the screaming and shouting rose from outside.

"Why are people screaming daddy?" Rose muttered, rubbing her tired eyes. Kyle looked out the window to see people streaming past the house towards the shoreline. Through the shouting and screaming Kyle heard "Fire! Fire!"

"Kyle come with me. Alistair stay here and keep your mother and sister safe." Tomen ordered as he strapped up his tool belt. A look of apprehension on Kyle's face as the chaos increased outside. "Kyle, we need to help, this is no time to be scared, grab your stuff."

As Kyle and Tomen ran through the village towards the shore, they could already see the towering fire in the distance. The fire had grown so large it rivalled the moons in the dark night. After a minute, they finally reached the edge of the village, just above the shouting of the people, Kyle heard a familiar voice. Scanning in the direction of Lucia's house, he saw her in the midst of an argument with her father.

For years her father had been aggressive towards her and her family. People in the village often suspected fouler things than just shouting although no one could prove it. There were times Lucia ran away from home, sometimes to Kyle, others times to the woods above the village. Each time she would return to try and protect her mother and sister.

"Stay here, it's no place for a girl!" Lucia's father barked as he pushed her back onto the porch. The force of the push knocked her to the floor. Kyle, seeing the violent push stopped him dead in his tracks as a stirring feeling of anger came over him. As the anger grew, so did a power inside him.

"Kyle, I need your help now." The sudden bark broke Kyle's trance. As suddenly as the feeling of power grew, it had faded away. Glancing over to his father to see him untying the boat, Kyle moved to help.

A few minutes and tugging and rigging the boat they were out onto the open water and sailing towards the monastery. Surrounding them were a dozen other boats, each different from the last, some as small as theirs, others large enough to take half the village. The towering fire on the island guided the boats toward the island, the light shimmered golden on the choppy water. An erry silence shrouded the boats as they continued sailing for fifteen minutes. Each minute felt like an hour as Kyle thought about Master Pret and the monks. For hundreds of years, they stood as the wisest people in the world and now they're monastery burns. The books, scrolls and items of a thousand years being consumed to ash in a single night.

Finally reaching the shore, the villagers were hit with intense heat from the fire. The deafening roar of the flames made it nearly impossible to hear the shouting to each other.

"Get the pump setup, everybody grab a bucket and start trying to get the fire under control." Even as Tomen shouted, barely anyone heard the orders. As everyone set about their duties, Kyle looked towards the entrance, his heart pounding in the chaos surrounding him. Just beyond the raging fire, a silhouette of a figure stood looking back at him. Covered entirely in black it's fixed gaze pierced through his soul as if all the life was draining from him. The figure continued to remain fixed on Kyle. A sullen weight fell on Kyle's mind, dulling his senses until a single thought remained.

Move, move, move.

As if in a trance Kyle felt his body slowly start to step forward. The flames whipped and cracked in the wind, the flaming snakes biting at Kyle's skin. A parting in the flames allowed Kyle to continue his slow march into the inferno. In the tunnel the smoke was so thick, every breath Kyle took was like breathing underwater, but still he marched towards the shadow.

Finally, he reached the courtyard and found some measure of relief from the unrelenting smog. The once beautiful green lawn now turned to black, the mighty oak that stood lively and resolute now lifeless and charred. Embers and ash from the branches and upper floors fell like grey snow in the wind. As the smoke cleared, so too did his vision as the first thing he saw was Master Pret laid clutching his chest as he dragged himself to the epitaph, the floor behind him coated thick in his blood.

"Master Pret." Kyle exclaimed as he clambered towards his mentor.

"What's happening, where is everyone else?" Before Pret could respond a dark figure moved in the corner of Kyle's limited vision. Stirring amongst the smoke like a ghost, the shape formed into many as they glided in the illuminated smoke.

"What is that?"

"Death." Pret sputtered. "They are the bringers of darkness and evil."

Kyle swiftly focused back on Pret who gripped his chest tighter. The silhouetted figures began to surround the courtyard, each one coming to a stop to form a barrier around the tree. Kyle couldn't see their faces, but he knew they were staring intently at him.

"We are the true bringers of light." The voice cut through the burning fire and Kyle, freezing him to the spot. Emerging from the smoke Keela held Master Pret's amulet. Each footstep kicked up embers from the smouldering grass surrounding him in fire. Kyle felt the burning heat turn to ice in his veins at the sight of Keela. "We will bring the true bringers of light, and from its ashes, *she* will bring peace to this world." Keela held up the amulet as a hunter with a trophy. His eyes fixed on the jewels surrounding the golden circlets. Kyle instantly recognised it and looked back to Master Pret. "It is unfortunate that you shall not live to see these events that are to come." In a calm manner, Keela signalled for the others to leave the burning courtyard. In unison every shadow faded into the smog leaving only the amber hue surrounding them. Over the cracking wood and crumbling stone, a distant voice of Tomen called out.

"Kyle! Where are you!" Kyle tried to speak, but the chill in his body choked the words in his mouth. Keela without hesitation turned and walked towards the corridor his followers had escaped down. Kyle watched as the flames retreated away from Keela as if in fear of being extinguished. After a moment the feeling of dread evaporated.

A hand fell firmly on his shoulder. Spinning round in panic to see Tomen staring back at him.

"Kyle you need to get out of here, now!" Tomen's voiced muffled from the water-soaked rag that covered his mouth. Tomen pulled on Kyle, but Kyle crouched firmly.

"We need to save the other monks. There could be others." Tomen knew Kyle had a point, the village had depended on the monks for centuries, if they were to thrive, they needed them.

"I'll try to look." Tomen pulled on Kyle harder. "You get out of here, now." Tomen took a deep breath in and moved across the fire scorched courtyard. A cough from Pret caused Kyle to turn and instinctually try to life Pret's lifeless body.

"No, it's no use my boy." Pret continued to cough violently. Blood pooled in his mouth and cascaded out of the corners. "It is too late for me."

"No, no I can still pull you free. I'll save you." The panic in Kyle's voice echoed. Pret grabbed firmly on his arm.

"I have one final task for you, one of which the fate of the world is at stake." The panic that was in Kyle's voice spread across his face.

"The people that attacked us seek to unleash an ancient and powerful being on the world, one which this order has gone to great lengths to keep entombed. You must take the icon to Artheria, to a scholar named Felix." The fire and smoke began to take its toll on Pret.

"But master, the man already has your icon, how can I defeat someone like him? I'm only one man?" The light in Pret's eye slowly began to fade.

"A man can change the world, as for the icon." Pret outstretched his arm towards the charred mighty Oak and with his last ounce of energy, blasted a force at the base of the tree. The force was enough to blow a section out of the husk to reveal a small chamber.

"The icon has been at the root of this order." Pret whispered. Stunned by the display of power, Kyle turned back to Pret, his eyes vacant and still. The overwhelming flood of emotions filled Kyle but with panic and fear, Kyle leapt toward the tree and dove his hand into the chamber. The sound of an almighty crack as the Oak tree began to wane under the weight. With no time to think Kyle pulled the Icon from the base and scrambled towards the exit as fast as he could. Each breath was agony as the smoke filled them. The tree started to crack and snap as it lent to one side. Finally, it gave way, landing like an earthquake behind Kyle, the path sealed.

Reaching the outside, the heat of the fire still reached his skin as Kyle made his way down the path. All the villagers that had come to help were retreating towards the boats as walls crumbled under the inferno. The last stand of the monastery was the tower of the master. Finally buckling, it gave way falling into the maw of the inferno.
"Father!" Kyle cried out as he looked on at the chao in front of him. A quick response called back. Kyle darted to look in the direction to see Tomen resting on a boulder a couple metres away. His face and hands were burnt and blistered, his breathing heavy.
"For a moment I thought you were still in there." Tomen still panting looked back at the hellfire he escaped from. His youth, family history and the village's ancestry raised to the ground within hours. A sadness fell in his heart he couldn't comprehend yet. Without a word, Tomen stood up and ushered for them to head back to the boats. As quickly as they ran to help, they were all back on the boats sailing home, each staring in disbelief at what they were witnessing. Tomen's demeanour had changed drastically since Kyle had last seen him.
"Father? Did you find anyone else?" Kyle staired as Tomen continued to focus on the dark sea beside him. For the rest of the night, both sat in silence, the horrors seared into their memories.

One by one the boats returned to an even greater sadness. Villagers stood upon shore, women clutching their children, husbands, brothers and fathers helpless as their livelihood faded into the darkness of the night. Alexia and the other children were no different, tears running down their faces. Kyle had never seen his mother cry before which for him made the night all the more heart-breaking. A single tear on her cheek turned into a drip and suddenly he felt something on his face. Raindrops started to fall on them, each spattering as they continued to grow in strength. Soon it fell harder on them all until it felt like a storm. Kyle looked up at his mother and instead of seeing her smiling face, she hung her head, eyes closed.

A Journey Decided
Chapter 7

It had been a couple of days since the fire on the island, and the village had been distraught at the 'accident'. The centuries since the village was founded nothing had come close to the horror of this tragedy and it showed. The cornerstone of their society had gone, and people walked through the town with almost a look of being dazed or lost. Kyle was the only one who knew the true cause of the fire, but he feared no one would believe anyone could attack the monks. Restless nights, reliving the nightmare kept flashing back but for those days Kyle didn't spend a lot of time indoors as he tried to avoid the sadness that fell upon his parents. For him it was painful but for his mother and father he couldn't begin to understand their sadness. The one thing in their lives that had been resolute, now lies ruined, the island now a graveyard.

Perched on a branch, Kyle sat staring out over Rheia, often thinking about it as a toy town upon the ground. He liked to imagine creating little stories of the people and playing them out in his mind, anything to distract him from the last couple of days. Being so far away on the borders of the Telloma forest he listened to the wind glide between the trees, rustling the branches. Today though he couldn't imagine his stories or dreaming of being the hero of his town, mighty Kyle the hero of Rheia. Instead his thoughts were of his teacher, Master Pret, the images of that night playing on his mind. In his hand, the last gift from Pret, a strange metal amulet. He guided his fingers over the raised impressions that ran in patterns between seven coloured stones. Kyle had never seen such a token never mind dreaming of ever holding something so rich. In the centre of the amulet, a triangular hole with grooves etched into the core. Why would Pret give it to him? Of all the treasure on the island, why this? Kyle thought for hours alone, hoping to figure it out.

"Be careful."

Kyle broke his stare to see Lucia smiling up at him. "I can see you thinking, that's dangerous." She said, making her way up the side of the tree. Kyle turned back to the amulet once more before hiding it in his trouser pocket. The mystery would have to wait. Clambering to sit on a branch nearby, She looked at him as Kyle turned his attention to her. He always admired her spirit. In the morning sun, her auburn hair shone splendidly as it flowed in the spring breeze. Kyle was constantly drawn to her eyes, emerald and as mysterious as the jewels that adored the amulet.

"I heard about Master Pret. I can't believe an accident like that could happen there; it was so peaceful there." The sincerity calmed Kyle, but it wasn't enough. The secret, the truth he knew ate at him day after day. If he couldn't tell an adult, he hoped that Lucia was the one person he trusted, would believe him.

"I don't think it was by accident."

"What do you mean?" Lucia asked, looking puzzled. Kyle knew how dangerous this could be, the idea that the attackers were looking for something.

"Think about Lucia, remember the stories Pret told us about the Dawning war, Nightshade? What if someone came looking for something?"

"But that was a thousand years ago? No-one is around anymore and I'm sure something like them were just stories." A quiet giggle in her voice, Kyle heard the ignorance in her voice. Playing with the amulet inside his pocket, unsure whether or not to tell her Pret's dying words, Lucia noticed Kyle's solemn demeanour didn't break under her innocent mood as he focused on something in his pocket.

"Kyle? You're beginning to make me nervous. The monks are peaceful, if someone wanted to take them why don't they just simply steal it without anyone noticing?"

Lucia was right, if they simply wanted it, stealing it quietly would be the best way, that's how he would do it. A darker thought crossed his mind.

"Maybe they were trying to send a message, or to distract people from following them."

The thought made him shudder. If these people could slaughter the monks, even those as powerful as Master Pret, there is no telling how far they would go to get what they wanted. Kyle saw the scepticism in her eyes.

"Come on!" Kyle snapped as he pulled out the amulet from his pocket. "Master Pret's necklace!"

"Yes, well not the one he wore. He gave it to me before he died. He said that I have to get it to Artheria, I'm sure the attackers were looking for this." Lucia stared at the jewelled amulet gleaming in Kyle's hand. It's seven jewels dispersing the morning light into rainbows on the tree bark.

"That's why I'm going to take it to Artheria." Kyle said, a heavy sigh on his breath. Kyle withdrew the artefact back to his pocket. Lucia's mouth gaped a little.

"You can't go. What about your family?"

"I have no choice, what if the attackers come looking for it here? I can't let them find it besides, Master Pret entrusted me to take it and deliver it to a scholar in Artheria."

As Kyle explained to Lucia, he struggled to convince himself of the journey. Waves of doubt came over him.

'What happens if I'm followed? Or worse.' No, he had to do this, his mentor trust him. He *must* have had a reason to do so.

"Maybe it's time I have my own adventure."

Lucia stared blankly at him. Kyle noticed the continued scepticism spreading across her face. "We've spent our whole lives listening to the tales of the past, heroes and their deeds, why not us? I want to do more than just fish and farm. Doing this I can see the world, look upon the tall towers of the Artherian academies, maybe see Telloma." An excitement sparked in his eyes at the thought of exploring the world beyond the boundaries of Rheia. "What about your family? Friends?" Lucia felt a lump in her throat, feelings longing to escape. The air changed as her gaze lingered on him. Kyle began to feel a rush of blood as a silence came over both of them. As they both stared into each other, the leaves on the branches began to sprout faster, each bud bursting from their cocoons, out stretching to the morning sun.

The distant sound of Kyle's mother Alexia called out to him from the valley. The moment broke as they both looked away. Lucia looked away bashful, her cheeks full and red. Kyle too was flushed, his heart pounding. He searched the valley for the voice, finally spotting a woman waving from an outlying house. Kyle looked back to Lucia who now looked away to the ground below. Reaching out, he placed his hand on hers in the hopes of rekindling the moment, but she moved her hand away.
"I should head back, father will be wondering where I've gone." Lucia said as she began her descent from the branch. A perfect moment fell to disappointment as he looked at the ground below before jumping. With a thud, landing on the soft ground before quickly standing. Kyle

turned to help Lucia down. Without a word they walk back towards the town. Determined not to leave his last moment with her soured, Kyle thought of the words to say.

"I'll still have a reason to come back." Kyle looked at her with a smile. Lucia didn't meet his gaze but instead smiled and walked towards her house. 'Now the hard part' Kyle thought as he walked back to his home.

Trial by Fire
Chapter 8

Kyle had spent the rest of the afternoon thinking about Lucia, his mind swarmed with memories of her, every detail but also of what was to come. The once sunny spring morning had turned to a continuous downpour of rain. All the colour in the world had faded in the grey light of day, but the thoughts of Lucia coloured his vision. Since they were children, Kyle always was drawn to Lucia, for better or worse they never seemed to be too far away from each other. That thought in itself gave him some strength since for the last couple hours Kyle played out the coming conversation, each time he struggled to understand even his own thoughts.

He ran through the images and words Pret had spoken to him before passing. Pret was his teacher, family and friend and the burden he was given overwhelmed him. He stood up and took in a deep breath.

The storm continued its unrelenting attack as wind collided with the house. A sudden rush of wind blew through the house rattling and shaking everything in its path. As the gust died, Kyle heard his father drop his tools by the side of the door. Since the night of the fire, Tomen had not been the same, his friendly attitude had been less of late remaining closed off to a lot of people. His wife Alexia, an always cheerful woman, still went about her day with a heavy heart. Each day some of the villagers had made the journey back to the island to check for survivors and for anything they could salvage. After just a few days the religious pilgrimage yielded less and less today, half burnt books, food that had survived and a couple relics.

Kyle had heard from another boy that the men had found a couple of bodies and buried them in the courtyard. Just the mention of the courtyard threw Kyle back into the nightmare, the dark messiah heralding his intentions sent a shiver down Kyle's back.

Low hushed voices pulled Kyle back to the present as he quietly made his way to the edge of the door to listen in on conversation.

"You must have found something." Alexia said with apprehension. For the first time in his memory, his mother had worry in her voice. "We have to recover as much as we can."

"We've been working day and night, each day we find less and less." Tomen replied sitting down in his chair. Kyle slowly peaked round the edge of the door to see a glimpse of them both sitting by the fire, leaning into each other like thieves.

"Did you find the icon at least?" Concern grew with every word.

"We checked everybody we could find, none of them had the amulet."

The mere mention of the amulet caused Kyle to grip the item in his pocket. 'What's so important about this amulet? How could this stop a demon from coming back?' Each time a question fired in his mind; a couple sprouted another in its place. Kyle's train of thought was broken by the continued whispering discussion by his parents.

"Ashoul and Vex will transport the relics we recovered in the morning. The journey should take a week."

Kyle looked closely at Tomen as he slumped back in his chair. "Can you still sense anything, a location to help us?" Kyle homed in on a glowing light from inside the palm of his mother. As the light slowly grew around her palm,

Alexia muttered under her breath. Kyle tried to hear the words but was too far away to make them out. The talk of amulets, relics and clandestine conversations between both of them made Kyle desperate to hear the incantation Alexia was performing. Never had Kyle seen his mother shown any abilities to use Mana and with such ease. Drawn in like a moth to a flame, Kyle took another step forward but failed to see the bucket at his feet. A loud knock as the bucket rolled into the doorway startling Tomen and Alexia. The incantation faded away as they both rose to their feet.

"Kyle, what are you doing back there? You shouldn't be up!" Tomen barked. His voice boomed through the wall as Kyle stepped forward.

"I know what you've been looking for." Kyle took another step closer to them. He saw the coy look on their faces as they tried to coerce more information.

"What do you mean you know what we're looking for?" Alexia asked. Kyle played around with the amulet inside his pocket as he tried to summon the courage to tell them.

"I know you've been looking for Master Pret's amulet and I know the monastery was attacked." Kyle saw a look of bewilderment on their faces. His mother looked at him with a little apprehension.

"How can you know any of this?" Alexia continued to ask. Kyle looked at Tomen who knew Kyle had some truth to his statement.

"My son, the incident at the monastery was nothing more than an accident." Kyle saw through the lie as he slowly began to pull out the amulet. It's golden circles and jewels glistened in the low fire light. Wide eyed, Tomen swiftly closed the distance between himself and Kyle and snatched it from Kyle's hand. In one motion Tomen handed the amulet to Alexia who started to mutter some unknown language.

"How did you get this? And how come you didn't tell me sooner; do you have any idea how serious this is?" Tomen snapped at Kyle. This was the first time Kyle had seen any sort of anger from his father which rendered him speechless. Both watched on as a layer of bright blue light swirled and began to encompass the amulet until it finally consumed it before fading away. Desperate for answers Kyle asked, "What is so important about that amulet?" Tomen shot a glare at Kyle.

"The protective spell should hold, but it might already be too late." Alexia worryingly spoke as she passed the amulet to Tomen. Frustration began to build in Kyle as Tomen continued to fixate of the amulet.

"Too late for what?" Kyle thought back to the final moments with Master Pret and the shadowy figure. "Does it have something to do with the *true bringer of light*?" Both instantly stopped what they were doing as if Kyle had insulted them.

"Don't you dare speak that phrase again." Tomen said raising his finger in pure authority. "I will not have dark scripture spoken in my house."

"How do you even know that passage?" A hint of curiosity grew in Alexia's voice.

"I don't care how he learnt it, I will not have it spoken again, you never know who might hear it." Tomen barked down at Alexia. The talking about it pushed Kyle's frustration until he finally burst out.

"I heard it from the people that attacked the monastery. One of them said that '*she*' will return and bring peace to this world."

"You saw who attacked the monks?".

Kyle shook his head in response. "I never saw his face, but Pret called them the 'Bringers of Darkness'." The name cut through them both as Kyle spoke it. "Who are they?" Alexia looked at Tomen for a moment until she finally looked back at Kyle.

"Are you familiar with the Dawning War?"

Kyle nodded.

"The Bringers of Darkness are called Shadow Blades. They were the servants of Nightshade, the sorcerer who summoned the demon Shassa to this world." Alexia continued. Each time she spoke, the thought of those shadows sent a shiver down Kyle's back. "Whenever they were seen, death was sure to follow. Since the defeat of Nightshade, they have long since disappeared, but it appears we were wrong. You are very lucky to have lived to see them." Kyle held back on worrying her about the rest of his account. He had heard of mysterious deaths from the stories people told drunkenly at gatherings, victims that seemingly could not have died yet did in brutal ways, but the reality of these Shadow Blades chilled Kyle.

"Master Pret gave me that amulet and told me to deliver it to a scholar called Felix in Artheria."

Tomen rolled his eyes at the notion.

"How could he task you with such a burden, you are a child, my child. You will not make it to Artheria if Shadow Blades are hunting you." Alexia remarked as she looked at Kyle. Kyle saw the doubt in their eyes but Pret had entrusted him, 'this is my quest' Kyle thought as he replied, "Mother, I'm sixteen years old, I'm not a child." Kyle could see his father had lost interest in Kyle's protest. "I can protect myself if I can use Mana.."

"... but you can't use it, Kyle!" Tomen interrupted. "You haven't the strength or the knowledge to use it at all. What you did on the boat was lucky and unfocused. If you use Mana without training it could hurt you, or worse, kill you." Tomen shook his head in disbelief. "No, I will take the amulet to Artheria, I know the way and I can protect it."

Kyle struggled to comprehend the seriousness of the events of the past days, the Shadow Blades and now the amulet. 'This must be a dream, a scary, horrible dream.' Kyle thought as if he had fallen into the pages of the many books he read. His thoughts soon turned back to the heroes of those stories. Each time they were scared, or they struggled to continue, they still had the courage to keep going. 'How can I be an adventurer if I can't even stand up to my father?'

"I have to do this, Master Pret entrusted me." Kyle spoke, the confidence in his mind wavered in his voice. A couple of screams from outside pieced through the heavy downpour. The screams were interrupted by the sound of smashing and yelling as the chaos grew closer. Each heard the faint but distinct sounds of swords clashing together as the screaming began to rival the patter of rain on the thatched roof. Tomen rushed without a word to a floorboard and pried it from the ground.

Diving his arm into the space below he quickly withdrew grasping a magnificent sword. Kyle had seen many swords in books, and some owned by the villager's, but many were dulled or chipped from their use and age. This was perfect, its long single edge was sharp enough to cut through the light as it bounced off the blade. Near it's tip the blade curved backwards and flattened out on the rear of the blade. The metalwork was exquisitely etched with images and runes unknown to Kyle, each one inset into the blade as black. The hilt was strapped and bound in black leather and finished at the pommel. The pommel was rounded but had a flat base to it. Kyle's eyes widened as he noticed the design on the base of the pommel was the same as the amulet, seven dots connected by lines.

"Stay here." Tomen spoke to Kyle before turning to Alexia. "Protect the amulet." Tomen leapt for the door and disappeared into the storm. The door swung wildly in the wind as rain spilled into the house. Kyle looked to his mother who rushed to pack a small bag ready for Tomen's return. Rose and Alistair began to whimper and cry at the chaos that raged outside. With her maternal instincts kicked in, Alexia left the bag to go protect her children leaving only Kyle and the amulet in the room. 'I have to get this as far away as possible from his family.' Kyle grabbed the rucksack and amulet and headed for the door.

From the moment he stepped outside, the smell of smoke lay in the air its smog limiting his vision. Even as the rain poured, the fires began to consume the houses. Kyle jumped down onto the ground, running only a few paces before instantly sticking in the waterlogged mud. Trudging through he finally found some dry patches, like stepping stones, he found a path easy enough to run on. The sound of swords clashing and people screaming grew louder as Kyle rounded a corner to see the dark hooded figures fighting some of the villagers. The Blades fought fiercely and with ease as they cut down the unprepared defenders. In the middle of the square Kyle watched as his father battled the same figure that spoke to him during the fire. Unlike the other hooded warriors his stance made him stand out. Upright and one handed he parried and deflected Tomen's advances with ease, like a cat playing with a mouse. Tomen jumped a couple steps forward with an almighty swing but missed. As quick as a blink the figure pivoted and sliced through Tomen's leg dropping him to his knee. Desperate to defend his village, Tomen staggered to his feet but to no avail. In another swift motion the figure had spun around and attacked his other leg felling his opponent. Tomen wailed in pain as he fell to his knees still grasping at his sword. Standing above Tomen, the figure towered over his victim, the rain now draining the blood into a nearby puddle.

Kyle moved to hide behind a nearby cart careful not to be spotted by the other Blades, he watched on as the last couple villagers fell to their attackers. The figure now pulled down his hood and mask to reveal a pale scarred face.

"I want you to know the face of your fate." He continued to look down on Tomen. "Keela, servant of Nightshade."

"No one here will give you what you seek." Tomen defiant as he held his legs. The figure turned his attention to the sword in Tomen's hand and snatched it away with ease. Sheathing his own sword, the figure held Tomen's weapon firmly in his hand inspecting the craftsmanship of the blade.

"Give me the amulet, and I shall leave this place." His voice was emotionless as he began to circle. Tomen didn't respond. His pride allowed him to brace himself for what was to come. Kyle looked on helplessly as Keela came to a stop behind his father.

"Very well." In one powerful motion the blade was forced through Tomen's back and out his chest before being wrenched out again. Tomen let out a pained gasp, blood already in his mouth.

"The time of your gods is over. The age of the true light has begun." Keela's voice boomed as if it came from the heavens itself. "If you will not yield then we will cleanse you from the earth!" Keela looked to his disciples, "Burn it all down."

Each one split off. Kyle watched on as one of the Blades sparked flames from his hand before launching it into the nearest building.

"Ariel." One of the Blades near to Kyle stopped and turn towards Keela. "Find the child." Without a sound Ariel silently moved into the village. Kyle noticed every footstep she took made no sound or impression upon the mud. Desperate to get to his father, Kyle gathered all the courage he had and prepared to move. Before he had a chance to move, he felt a hum emanating from his pocket. Curiously, Kyle placed his hand into his pocket to feel the amulet vibrating as if being struck like a tuning fork.

"I feel the amulet is nearby, find it my champion." A hissed voice screeched through the rain as Kyle looked for the source. Circling Keela, who now stood alone and in an almost trance state was a formless cloud. "Do not disappoint me again, or I shall need a new champion."

"It will be found my lord." The authority of a moment ago, was now stripped away to nothing as Keela addressed the formless shadow. "What of the child my lord."

The shadow came to a stop behind Keela. From the nothingness an arm, then hand formed as it outstretched to his head and neck. Kyle watched as if a puppet master playing with its creation.

"Bring him to me." It hissed. Without another word, the shadow forced its way back inside Keela through any opening on his head. The sudden rush caused him to stagger before he returned to his authoritative demeanour.

After watching Keela continue his search, Kyle pushed down all the fear that crippled him to the spot as he checked around him before leaving his hiding place. Quickly moving to his father who remained motionless in a pool of his own blood, all his emotions overwhelmed him. Shaking his lifeless body, tears began well up in his eyes before cascading down his cheek. Distraught and in despair Kyle looked at the sword that lay half buried in the mud, it's blade glinting in the firelight. On the curved blade the runes that decorated it glowed a dim red hue as it captured the firelight.

"He's here." A voice shouted from behind him. Running as fast as he could, Kyle in a panic lifted his sword. Its weight wasn't something Kyle expected as he battled to raise it. The man bared down on him was suddenly struck in the side with an almighty whirlwind force that threw him into a burning building. In shock Kyle saw Alexia standing with her hand raised, the rain soaking her to the bone.

"Kyle, run!" she shouted as more masked attackers closed on him. Kyle glanced at them before darting back to his mother. "Just go." Grasping the sword tightly for a moment he battled with the idea of standing his ground, but the will of his mother won out. Kyle turned and began to sprint with all haste out of the village and towards the treeline above. His years of playing and running up and down the hills gave him an advantage over his pursuers as he galloped up the hill and into the trees.

With every step he took into the forest, the light began to fade as the trees thickened. Their overhanging branches loomed over him casting darkness. As he dashed through the thicket, the bushes scratched and clawed at his clothes, each time leaving their mark on him. Undeterred, the Blades weren't far behind him. Kyle glanced over his shoulder to see dancing shadows jumping between the trees, he knew they would eventually bear down on him. After a couple minutes Kyle came upon a gully that led down into a stream. With the light from the stars and moons limited, Kyle could not see the bottom, only catching a glimpse and sound of the trickling water. Only a moment had passed but the Blades had caught up to him, as two dived at him. By the force of the impact all of them tumbled head of heels down the hill until they splashed into the water. The impact was sudden and hard but the ice-cold water cleared Kyle's mind as he rose in shock. The two Blades were already to their feet, their weapons drawn.

"Leave me alone!" Kyle shouted, swinging his sword desperately. "I don't have anything."

"Who says we want anything?" One of the men said, his voice was deep and broken. "Our master wants you, so he shall have you." Lashing out the man's sword caught Kyle's arm lightly. The Blade stung like a bee as he withdrew and started to circle around Kyle.

"Give it up Kid, maybe the master will make it quick for you." The other voice spoke. His was lighter and oddly soft. "Just like your fathers."

The words cut through Kyle who tried to keep all his emotions down with every fibre of his being. Master Pret had spoken about a warrior's ability to suppress their emotions during battle, Kyle however was no soldier. A torrent of emotions flooded his mind as he started to feel the tingling sensation, he had felt only a few times before. This sensation was different however, it grew in strength quicker than ever until a slight light started to emit from his veins. The two Blades stopped and were stunned by the growing display of power until the wash of anger took control of Kyle. As the rage took him, Kyle screamed at the top of his lungs before striking the ground with his fist. An overwhelming blue wave expelled from his body and knocked the two pursuers with such force they were thrown back up the gully. The rage subsided as quickly as it built. Kyles's breath was laboured and deep as he staggered to his feet. Kyle could only hear the patter of raindrops on the leaves by him but even they felt different. The drops tingled on his skin, steam sizzled back into the air. It felt as if all the life and energy had drained from his body as he slowly placed one foot in front of the other.

Time appeared to blur in his mind as Kyle slowly staggered through the forest with only his instinct to push him further. After a while Kyle made it to a clearing in the trees. The rain had stopped and given way to the moons that shone down on him. The smell of fresh dew on the grass had replaced the burning ash and flesh of his village. With nothing left to move, Kyle collapsed to his knees then onto his back. Tiredness had finally won out as he closed his eyes.

Flashes of images flew through Kyle's mind. A mountain surrounded by smoke, a city in flames and people he had never seen fighting waves of creatures. Finally, he woke atop a cliff overlooking the sea. The far cry feeling dread and fear washed away by the sounds of the sea crashing against the cliffs. Standing out overlooking the sea, a woman dressed in a light blue dress, her hair adorned with flowers that led up to a crown of branches and flowers. Kyle tried to sit up but was locked in place as if a weight had been placed on his chest.

"Kyle" The woman whispered, her voice carrying on the wind like a sweet song. Kyle recognised the voice from when he was fishing with his father. "Protect the key for you are destiny of many."

Kyle fixed on the woman as she began to turn. A gust of wind blew past and much like her voice, the woman faded on the wind until she had disappeared leaving him alone.

Marching on to Destiny
Chapter 9

The gentle sound of a breeze roused Kyle from his rest. As he opened his eyes, he saw the tops of the trees flowing freely against the backdrop of a pure blue sky. Around him the echoes of wild birds chirping filled him with calm, a feeling he had not felt in some time. As he sat up, the meadow surrounding waxed and waned in the light breeze that swept through it. His body was tender and throbbed.

Lying next to him, the sword of his father brought back the fresh feelings and moments of last night, the horror of seeing his village in flames, friends and neighbours lying dead in the waterlogged mud. His mind fixated on the image of his father knelt before the shadowed figure, the sword running through his back and out his chest. A sudden feeling of loneliness came over him as he finally stood up. Every muscle in his body continued to ache and twitch, it hurt as more than anything he had felt in his life. With only a small supply of food, Kyle quickly ate whatever his mother had managed to pack before gathering his things and setting out on his journey. He still wasn't sure how far he managed to trudge through the forest after fending off the Blades. By his reckoning, if he travelled the road to Artheria, he could arrive in three days, but the road would undoubtedly be watched. The safest way was to cut through the forest and hope he could use the trees to cover his tracks. For hours Kyle trekked through the outlying forest of Telloma occasionally the trees broke into a rocky outcropping or ravine. After a day of walking the trees soon came to an abrupt end on the banks of a small river that flowed to the sea. He was finally at the boundary of his village's influence, none of his friends had ever ventured as far as he had. This sudden thought made his chest sink, the realisation he has no idea what awaits him beyond the river. Maybe his father was right, maybe he wouldn't be strong enough to make the journey to Artheria. Kyle looked down and pulled out the amulet from his bag and stared at it before glancing at the river, the surface glinting in the light. The power of the river looked strong enough that it might carry him away or even the amulet. 'Maybe it could carry it to the sea then it would be lost forever.' The Kyle thought loosened his grip. A fear grew in the pit of his stomach at the thought of losing his father and maybe his mother, the thought of never seeing his family or even Lucia. Kyle took a step forward and prepared to throw it, but something halted him. An echo in his head rang out, drowning out all thoughts until only a single remained. An image of Master Pret sat on the stone bench in the monastery's courtyard. On his lap laid a heavy thick book opened. Kyle flashed a glimpse of the page, a city of a thousand towers on the sea, Artheria. Master Pret looked up from the book and smiled at Kyle. The sound rang out again but this time it focused into the voice of Master Pret. Kyle's mentor never spoke, but instead felt his words

"Continue on my boy, no hero's journey is ever easy. You will soon find your destiny in this world." Pret raised his hands and clapped. The clap pushed Kyle back and within a moment he was back on the riverbank with the amulet in his grasp.

'Halfway there and no sign of the blades' Kyle thought 'I need to do this' as his resolve returned to him. Crouching behind some reeds he scanned both sides of the river before crossing. After wading through a narrow section of the river, Kyle spent a day and night travelling the forest finding rest under rocky overhangs and large trees, ever watchful of who might be following. One day Kyle had managed to climb a hill that was in front of him. Using the roots and trunks of the mighty Oak and Birch trees that covered the hill, Kyle could feel his legs scream in agony at the continuous march uphill until he finally reached the crest. He had gone on adventures with Lucia and the other children but never climbed hills as tall or steep as this one. As he stood above the valley, below Kyle could see the ocean in the distance. The blue water stretched out to the very farthest horizon from the east all the way to the west and at the centre of the shoreline, mighty golden walls stood. Artheria, 'The city of knowledge' Pret had called it to him and the other children. The golden sandstone walls enclosed a massive city filled with houses, academies, libraries, and everything in between. Scholars from around the known world from as far as the desert cities of Tillait travelled to learn the mysteries of the world. His imagination had been so small, even with the help of the books from all corners of the known world, nothing had prepared him. Kyle thought about the journey he had taken, his 'heroic quest'. It was not what he had expected. Turning back in the direction of his village Kyle saw faint plumes of smoke rising front behind the treeline. Everything he was doing, he was doing it to protect them. That simple fact in itself was enough.

Kyle rested on the crest for an hour, allowing for his legs to recover from the arduous trek. Beside him laid his father's sword, the last remaining gift from Tomen. He chewed on the last remaining provisions that had been packed into the bag. A small loaf of bread was all he had, his stomach growled as it set to work on the final crumbs it had been fed. The quiet chatter of the animals was disrupted by the falling of rocks behind him. Like a skittish rabbit, Kyle leapt to his feet holding the sword. His eyes darted around looking for signs of his attackers but the only movement he saw was a couple of rocks that had rolled off a larger outcropping. Thinking his eyes had started to play tricks on him from exhaustion, a couple of the rocks had started to move slowly. Kyle stared at the outcropping as he tried fix on the movement but after a few minutes he resigned to his mind's delusions. As he sat down Kyle thought to one of the fairy tales his mother told him as a child about the Bjargmen, the stone men, were creatures that were made of rocks and could grow to the size of castles. Kyle always imagined meeting one, but Tomen had always dismissed them as no one had ever met one before. With all the rest he could spare, Kyle gathered his possessions and pushed on towards the glittering city below.

The City of a Thousand Towers
Chapter 10

After a few hours hiking down the hill, Kyle finally reached the border of the great forest and into the plains between. In the distance Artheria stood like a glimmering jewel in the midday sun. Kyle pulled out his water sack and drained the last few drops from it. Savouring the water, he set out on the last few miles towards the city gates. As he drew nearer the wall grew ever more impressive and grander. Even from a distance Kyle could make out ornate cravings etched into the walls, pictographs and verses of the city's histories exposed for all the worldly elements. On the northern side stood a great bronze gate standing higher than any building he'd ever seen. Wide enough to allow two large carts to pass through and space for people as well, its size was only matched by its grandeur. On the face of it, epitaphs the city's founder Arturus and other nobles that built the city stand guard.

Finally reaching the gate to the city Kyle stood in marvel at the scale. The wall stretched as far west and east as he could see, guards lined the wall and protected the gates. Nobles and lesser folk passing through the gates talking, working or travelling. A few of the noblemen and women were carried on raised seats to avoid the muddied ground under the gates. If the walls hadn't convinced Kyle of the age of the city the roads leading in certainly did, mud and rocks had been trudged up under feet of thousands of people. Tents and stalls lined the main road leading into the city, merchants desperate to sell their wares to anyone passing. Still in awe, Kyle made his way through the gate to a new world. The streets were packed full of people from all walks of life. On most of the street corners preachers of knowledge or religion gathered in debate. The streets lined with buildings of different shapes and sizes, some tall, small, wide or narrow. Each one had its own character, built new or on top of older buildings, but like the glimmering beacon, each one wasn't dirty or dilapidated but instead they were tidy and in good condition. Kyle came to a stop at a crossroads as one philosopher posed a debate to a crowd of citizens. His regal red robes were of a fine cut far superior to the people that he stood above.

"Idella, the mother of the world has not forsaken us! She lives and resides in all of us." The preacher spoke, his hands raised in prayer to the group. A couple mutter to each other.

"Idella has left us. If she is the protector of us but then why does she do nothing when my farm was raided?" One man shouted. Kyle focused in on the man, his skin was of an old farmer, sun beaten and leathery. An old, healed scar lay across his brow. The preacher did not look at him but to the whole street.

"Idella teaches us that protection starts with ourselves. Idella does not give you courage but rather gives you opportunities to be courageous. She does not give us wealth or fortune but again gives us the chances to find these things." He proclaimed before turning his gaze to the man, "Idella is with us always, she is on the wind, the water and in our hearts, all you need to do is listen."

The words were like lightning in Kyle's mind, sparking him to continue on his task. Walking on he looked around at the new world marvelling at everything. In the distance he could see the city rising towards the cliff tops, the odd spire rising over the tops of the buildings and in the centre, the grand palace, home to the heirs of Arturus himself.

Kyle had learnt from the monks about the lineage of the two great houses although he always struggled to remember their names. Xaria was Lord of Artheria and had been for nearly eighty years. In the time of his rule Xaria had spent his life learning the ways of Mana and had amassed such a knowledge it was said his veins coursed with bright blue. Pret had also gone on to tell him that Mana had an unusual ability to prolong the lives of those who dedicate themselves to its mysteries.

The other major city in the north was Beltoria. Pret hadn't talked about it much other than it was the seat of power for the line of Bellatris. The soldiers were fierce and dedicated to their craft. After a few moments Kyle realised his quest had only just begun. 'How am I going to find Felix in this place?' he thought as sat down on a nearby step.

The Sleight of Hand
Chapter 11

Chanting, laughing and the smashing of bottles were the usual sounds of the day in the tavern Domina frequented. 'Easiest marks are the drunks' she always knew as she sat near a corner of the tavern. The place was filled with nobles and common folk alike. Money didn't mean much in a place like this. Drink and women, or men depending on the fancy, were the only things that each class had in common.

As much as she felt disgusted by it, she sat with grace as Domina played with her clothes to attract an easy target. Her long dark hair draped over her shoulder, resting gently on her chest. A slender beauty with olive skin, it wasn't long before she had a bite and lucky the man she had been tracking for a while. A slightly overweight man dressed in clothes that had long since lost their nobility. Dirt had stained the edges of the sleeves, the stitching fraying across his tunic. 'Not much a prize, but a prize no the less' She thought as he staggered his way over to her, slumping into the chair beside her, splashing ale about the table as he did.

"There you go my jewel." He hiccupped as he took a large mouthful ale. Domina pushed down her disgust at the unsightly man after hearing the ring of coins from the purse on his waist. She quickly unlaced another part of her tunic to reveal a bit more cleavage. Flicking her hair, she changed her character to seductive.

"Thank you, I got to say, what's a big strong man like you doing in Artheria?" She asked all the while playing up her 'assets'.

"I'm here on business" He responded, hiccupping further. His attention falling down from her face. "My father sent me to seal a trade with another family." He tried to sit up with authority, but his balance had long since failed him. "My family is a great house of the north and by this day's end we will be the wealthiest in the north." Her eyes widened at the prize although not surprised and the forthcoming of information. Men had been easy to manipulate for her, drink and seduction were easy to use, failing that she always played to their pride.

"So, you'd be as rich as the king of Beltoria?" She whispered softly to him.

"Well not as rich as the Lord of Beltoria." He piped up. "Long live Lord Algah!" he shouted in patriotism. A few fellow kinsmen shouted in return at the remark before downing their drinks. Seeing a perfect opportunity, Domina slowly began to reach for his purse. Her fingers snaked across his rotund belly as he continued to down the drink. Her face grew closer to his as she reached her fingertips on the string. The nobleman slammed down his mug to see her closing in on him. His infatuation grew as he licked his lips.

"You are a forward one aren't you?" He said. Domina saw the look of lust in his eyes. The string finally came loose as she continued the ruse. He moved in for a kiss, but she withdrew smiling. "You are a tease; I like that in a woman." He turned his body to face her.

"Yeah, but you'll have to find someone else." All the seductiveness vanished from her leaving only the disgust she had held back. Confused about the sudden change he grabbed at her arm. "If it's a question of pay, I have more than enough for a night." He fumbled to find his coin purse.

"I'm not someone to be bought." She said angrily. For years she had a problem with the nobles 'owning' another person, her reply dripped with venom. "Find someone else." As Domina turned to walk away the nobleman's grip tightened on her wrist.

"You stole my money!" he growled. His drunken state fuelled his anger. "I will have you for this and when I'm done, you'll wish you never crossed me."

"Ah well" She replied whimsically "Worth a try." In one quick motioned Domina forced the man's head down onto the table with a thud. The tavern fell silent as the nobleman laid still against the table. Looking up Domina saw all the drunken faces looking at her.

"What? He wanted a fight." She announced to the tavern, "I guess I won."

The common folk and some nobles roared with laughter and cheers at the remark. Some of the nobleman's kin however failed to see the funny side as they stood up. Domina slipped the coin purse into her tunic as she started to lace up. The men made their way towards her with purpose, shoving anyone out the way. Domina looked at the intimidating group and with a coy manner said, "Come on fair noblemen, you wouldn't hit a woman, would you?" The men remained unphased by the question as it was already decided. As quick as a cat, Domina ran for the door knocking a patron on the way out. The burly men stumbled for the door, each one knocking the other to get ahead.

Domina ran down the street a little further with the men only moments behind her. Dashing between the crowds of people with grace she ran down an alleyway between two houses. She made her way until a large wall blocked the rest of the alley. She was trapped. "How did this happen?"

She muttered to herself looking at the wall. "I'm smarter than this." Turning around, the three men had blocked the way out of the alley as they began their slow march towards her with ill intent. Darting her vision around for an escape. A group of baskets sat tucked up to the wall with washing lines and windows above them.

"Nowhere to go little girlie." One of the men said. His bumbling words felt slow and as dim-witted as he looked.

"No one gets away with stealing from Lord Dracos." Another said, this one's statue was a man of intelligence rather than brawn. "Give us the money and we shall be inclined to let you live."

The men came to a stop only a few metres away, two at the ready while the man in the middle remained more reserved. Domina had already made her play out in her mind. Taking a couple steps forward, the leader of the three raised his hand, readied for the money. Domina smirked at the three as she about faced and lept forward with her cat-like grace skipped up the baskets and bounded off the building wall to grab the adjoining wall. The three men stood in amazement as Domina effortlessly sat upon the wall looking down at them.

"Nice try fellas" Domina laughed looking down at them, "I'd give you a coin for your effort, but I don't want to." Domina jumped down the other side of the wall and vanished into the crowds.

Sat on a rooftop Domina continued to count the money she had earnt. With every coin that jingled in her purse a feeling of satisfaction came over her. 'Not bad for a morning.' She thought looking down on the potential marks below. All of them looked so small and hard-working, in her experience these were the ones that didn't have much worth taking to begin with. It was the ones who had a certain walk to them, a superiority about themselves. She didn't like having a code, they only got in the way, but at the same time she never liked to take away from those who had little. Amongst the crowds she spotted a young man looking lost as he walked along the street.

"Country boy" She muttered to herself, they always had the same bearing as each other, head footed and wide eyed. 'Probably from all the working in the fields and seeing something bigger than their tiny lives' she thought. Every now and then he stopped someone to ask something. Intrigued by him, Domina focused in on the boy as he moved closer.

"Excuse me but can you help me? I'm looking for a man called Felix." Kyle asked but to no avail. The crowd ignored him as they continued about their business. Undeterred Kyle continued to ask people until a group of academics stopped.

"Please can you help me, I'm looking for a man called Felix?" Kyle asked one of the scholars. The dark-skinned scholar was dressed in a cream robe with an emblem of fire on arm as did the rest of his company. These were scholars from alchemy academy, strange folk who played with rocks to create unwieldly inventions.

"Felix? I know a few called Felix. You may have to be more specific in a city such as this." He said with a smile.

"He deals with Master Pret from the monastery on the island of Ault.".

A look of scepticism crossed the man's face.

"You are looking for Felix of the Cyrillian order?" he responded.

"Yes, that must be him." Kyle replied, 'finally a spark of good news' he thought.

"I know where he is, follow the road down to the bazaar and take a left, you will see his house on the left. Look for a seven-pointed crest etched on the door". The man continued to look confused by the request. "I must warn you though, he is quite… strange." A couple of the scholars chucked as they turned and continued on their way. With the guidance of the man, Kyle made his way down the street. Domina, now satisfied with her choice, made her way along the rooftops following him, eager to see what he had to take.

The Cyrillian Order
Chapter 12

The hustle and bustle of the busy street fell silent as the large cracked doors closed behind him. The bright sunlight that had blinded his vision before was now obscured by towers of books, papers and dust that littered the room with only beams of light creeping through. For a moment Kyle imagined he had stepped into a future of what his home might look like if he continued to collect books.

As Kyle's eyes adjusted, the room came into focus and before him he saw what was once a grand staircase. It's marble stairs, stone spindles and handrails were all cracked and chipped from years of neglect. The carpets had not fared much better, the edges frayed, and moth eaten and the colour long since faded. As he scanned the surrounding rooms, he realised all the once majestic house had fallen out of time.

"Hello?" Kyle called out.

His voice echoed around the house. The echo lasted so long he thought someone had called back to him. "Is anyone here? I'm looking for a man called Felix." The echoes began to jumble as it bounced around the building. Kyle started to walk about the place, hoping to find someone to ask. Each room was similar to the last, piled high with books and paper, dust and most of all devoid of life. In many ways this was a dream for Kyle, the knowledge and stories contained within all these books was enticing to him, but he thought, it could also be a glimpse into a possible future for himself, so far it wasn't as appealing as he thought. If he continued to collect books for his own collection, he'd end up like crazy old man Paloa from the village. Kyle didn't think he was crazy, funnier than anything, but the village had labelled him crazy after he tried to capture lightning into a bottle to use. He was convinced it was the only way people without the ability to use Mana could finally use it. Kyle had a quick chuckle at the memory when Paloa told the village his idea.

High above Kyle amongst the wooden rafters, Domina had managed to sneak in through a small broken window. Balancing on the rotten beams she stalked Kyle as he moved between the rooms. As he looked around what he thought was a study, a large, bronzed statue stood covered in dust, but it's appearance held onto its dignity. Its face was of a man rigid and broad and was dressed in robes with pieces of armour covering his chest, shoulders, forearm and shins. The armour was exquisitely decorated with stones and inlays of gold and silver. In one hand was a knife, curved and a dragon upon its hilt, in the other sat a glowing rough stone. Kyle was memorized but the shifting colours the stone emitted, almost goading him into touching it to which he almost obliged until a quiet shuffle scratched on the floor behind Kyle.

Turning to see the source of the shuffle, an old somewhat frail man appeared from behind a mountain of books. His robes were simple and plain, a long scraggly beard was long enough to reach his belly; however, his hair had thinned on top. Even in the low light of the room Kyle could see the thinness of his skin, the old man's bones showing through clearly. The old man muttered under his breath as he read a scroll in his hands.

"Hello, are you Felix?" Kyle asked, moving forward towards the man. He continued to ignore and mutter to himself. A feeling of unease slowly started to rumble in Kyle as he approached the old man.

"Hello? I said I'm looking for a man called Felix. Does he live here?" Kyle was now stood next to him as the man continued to be oblivious. Kyle raised his hand and placed it on the elderly man's shoulder.

"Oh" the man shouted, dropping the scroll and jumped back a few paces, his hands raised in what looked to be an awkward fighting stance. "In the name of Idella, who are you?" The man began to mumble to himself under his breath.

"I'm sorry to scare you, my name is Kyle." The man continued to stand ready, but to do what Kyle hadn't a clue. "I'm looking for a scholar named Felix, I was told he lived here."

"Felix? Felix!" He returned almost confused by the name.

"Yes Felix, do you know where I might find him?"

"Well yes of course I do, he's right here." The man relaxed as he stood up straight as if in pride. 'He?' Kyle thought.

"You are Felix?"

"Well of course I am, who else is it going to be?" He statue fell as he returned to his slouched position. He began to grumble to himself, cocking his head to the side.

"Well, it's not going to be anyone else is it." He snapped, twisting his head the other direction. Kyle jumped at the sudden outburst.

"I'm sorry, I didn't mean to offend." Kyle apologized, stepping back. The elderly man looked at him, his demeanour changed, more rigid and upright but welcoming face.

"My dear boy, you need not apologise for your offence, none was taken." The man said calmly. Confusion ran across Kyle's face at the sudden change in attitude. Kyle quickly looked around to see if anyone else was about, anyone else that might be able to help.

"If you are looking for Felix you need not look any further, I am Felix." Felix offered his hand, "How may I be of assistance?" Kyle smiled but still cautious, he raised his hand meet Felix and shook.

"I was sent by Master Pret from the monastery on Ault to deliver something, he said I must not deliver it to anyone else." Felix nodded and quietly began to walk towards a table buried under mounds of scrolls. Domina still high above listened in on the conversation, the chance to see a valuable item was intriguing, taking it would be even better. She began to slowly move across the beams, silent and perfectly balanced.

"Intriguing let me see what it is." Felix asked, moving the scrolls to the side. His serenity began to crack as he muttered. "Not now, we have a guest."

"I'm sorry?" Kyle asked. Felix appeared calm again for a moment.

"It's nothing to worry about, please show me what it is you have brought."

The suspicious behaviour made Kyle uncomfortable with each passing moment. Both locked eyes on each other, Felix waiting patiently for the item, Kyle trying to work out desperately what was going on. Pret must have known who Felix was and trusted him enough to send Kyle on this quest. As that thought simmered in Kyle, his apprehension slowly eased as he hesitantly pulled the amulet out of his pack and placed it on the table. Felix's eyes widened at the sight of the amulet. The floating dust settled around it, avoiding the golden object.

"Well, this is indeed an object of importance." Felix raised his hand, the temptation to touch was overwhelming, "The Amulet of Bellatris."

The name shocked Kyle. The realisation that he had been holding an item that belong to one of the greatest heroes in history. Silently in the shadows, Domina too began to salivate at the sight of such a prize. She continued to stare like a magpie to a shiny object.

"The Amulet of Bellatris, I thought it belonged to the king of Beltoria?" Kyle asked puzzled.

"A common mistake and one that the Cyrillian Order has held in secret for centuries." The urge to hold the item overpowered Felix as he finally picked up the item. Inspecting the intricate details of its design and aura, his fingers worked across the runes carved on its surface. Kyle had heard the story of the Dawning war from Master Pret for as long as he remembered, nearly every detail etched in his mind, but there was never a mention of the Cyrillian Order.

"Who are the Cyrillian Order?" Kyle asked. He noticed a symbol on the robe of the old man, seven stars joined together and at its centre a triangle. The symbol was similar to one that was carved into the epitaph in the monastery. "Master Pret was a member of the Cyrillian Order?" Felix placed down the item with great care.

"It's safe to say Pret trusted you with this item so I shall extend the same courtesy." Felix turned around and began to search through a stack of books nearby. "When Nightshade was defeated and Shassa driven back into the void, the remaining Lightbringers along with Bellatris and Arturus imprisoned Nightshades' essence into a stone tomb." Kyle watched on in surprise as Felix returned with a small cracked leather-bound book. Its cover was plain with only a small crest impressed into the spine.

"I remember Master Pret telling us the story of the Dawning war. He said Nightshade was defeated."

"Not entirely." Felix interrupted as he thumbed the pages. "His physical form was destroyed, but when he was cursed by Shassa, his spirit was split in two. Half of his spirit is bound to this realm whilst the other is connected to Shassa."

Kyle looked down at the drawings in the book. The rough sketches were of a design similar to the amulet of Bellatris. Each stone of the amulet fitted into each slot on the golden ring.

"That's enough, you're talking to much!" Felix immediately snapped again, so much so, Kyle jumped back in surprise but noticed Felix had snapped at himself.

"Shush, I am in control and the boy needs to know." Felix looked back at Kyle and smiled before returning his focus back to the book. The whole situation was both confusing but worrying. Maybe this might not be the person Pret meant, after all bleeding out and close to death, Kyle heard people often said strange things.

"What Pret probably didn't tell you was the toll the battle had taken on the twins." Kyle focused on Felix as he pointed to each stone, "Exhausted of their power, the remaining Lightbringers used the last of their power to seal Nightshade into his tomb. Each one of the heroes took a stone from their weapons and imbued it with their essence and hid them."

"So that's why they attacked." Kyle muttered to himself. Felix shuddered uncontrollably before demeanour.

"Who attacked! Speak boy!" Felix snapped, his voice now scratched and dry, "Speak up!"

"Who are you, what is happening to you?" Kyle reached for the amulet, but Felix released a spark of bright blue lightning from his hand. Kyle jumped back at his display. An internal struggle raged as Felix shuddered for a moment and returned back to an upright calm manner.

"Forgive my outburst, it's a symptom of my... condition, but I must know of whom you speak."

"What's wrong, who are you speaking to?" Kyle stood firmly, his hand instinctively on the pommel of his sword.

"Myself, I'm afraid this condition is of my own making." Felix exhaled as he glanced at the bronzed statue in the corner. "One of which there is no return." Felix looked back to Kyle, desperation in his eyes.

"What happened?"

"I tried to prove to my colleagues about the nature of Mana, unfortunately I didn't expect what happened, to happen. Now I am exiled to this place, forever."

For the next hour Kyle and felix retired to a quiet study with armchairs as he recounted the last week of events to Felix as Domina remained in the shadows above. Every word solidifying her interest. Keela and his Blades, the burning of his village did nothing to shock Felix.

"I am sincerely sorry for your loss but if what you say is true then we are indeed in trouble." Felix picked up the amulet and extended it to Kyle. "You must take it north, to the city of Beltoria, from there a colleague of mine shall take it from you."

"I can't go to Beltoria, I have to return to my family." Kyle explained as he pushed the amulet back to Felix. "I did what Pret asked of me, I don't know the way." Kyle hesitated. For the longest time Kyle had dreamt of being on a hero's quest but now he was on his own, dread and doubt filled him. Thoughts of his village, family and Lucia flashed through his mind. "You must take it; I'm giving you it."

"I cannot take it, I'm in no condition to make the journey." Felix sat down in a worn armchair near a grand fireplace.

The armchair was surrounded by more stacks of books, each one of the cracked and worn from years of use. "Master Pret entrusted you with this quest to bring it to me, so he will have seen a strength in you. The same strength that I know will help you in the events to come."

A Nightmares Wrath
Chapter 13

Searing pain streaked across Keela's mind as he fell to his knees in agony. His veins blackened across his body as he continued to writhe in pain. Scattered around him the formless being swirled engulfing Keela. The forest around them was dark from the night but the light itself hid from the presence of the being. Keela pleaded with the spectre. "Forgive me master." Letting out a yelp, "The icon slipped out of our reach." The spectre let out a screech that could rival a banshee.

"Fool, I do not care for your mistakes!" it lashed out at Keela causing him more pain, "You are but a pawn, in an ever-growing game."

Keela fought to raise his eyes to the shade.

"You are a god, why do you need this trinket?" He asked as he continued to absorb the pain. His grunts had not gone unnoticed by Ariel who sat amongst the shadows of the bushes. Every lash and whip the being gave caused her to flinch, if even for a moment. Her leader, her love, a once strong and powerful man brought to his knees by a ghost. "Because I command it!" the ghost struck out, a phantom limb now wrapped around his neck. The black veins now burned red like fire as he let out a scream of agony. Ariel thought back to the first time she saw the spectre and Keela's orders. 'Never get involved my love, he is a god.' He spoke. Unable to take the screams of anguish Ariel sprung from the shadows. As she sprinted towards the shadow, she drew her blade.

"Ariel, no!" Keela let out, his voice cracked as he struggled to breathe. It was too late. Quicker than a flash, the being had wrapped another phantom limb around Ariel's throat.

Dropping to her knee's she looked on at Keela. The phantom let out another shriek, this time the being released its grip, but the piercing sound caused both to claw at their ears. The formless cloud expanded around them both until all was in darkness inside.

"A pity you do not have the guile of your underling," The voice whispered. The words bounced and echoed around them as if they were surrounded. "You may have taken the amulet without a single person knowing but your arrogance made you weak."

"I struck fear into those that would oppose Shassa." Keela spoke as he raised his head pride at his actions.

"Enough!" the voice shouted, "Do not try to comprehend something out of your understanding."

"What is her plan my lord?" Ariel whispered. Keela shot her a look as she spoke. The cyclone that had enveloped them suddenly retreated into a single shape of a man. As it morphed, legs began to take shape as it took a step forward. Despite its spectral being it seemed to struggle to keep upright, staggering with every step.

"The one true goddess of this world will fulfil the prophecy that has been hidden since the dawn of time." The being finally came to a stand above Ariel. Looking up, Ariel finally saw the face of death. The phantom's face was warped and scarred, it's eyes glowed blue as it gazed down upon her. It raised its hand and placed it onto Ariel's head. Keela looked on helplessly as Ariel experienced a vision. The visions overwhelmed her as Ariel let out a cry of her own until she collapsed in exhaustion and convulsing.

"The world will know Shassa's arrival as the rising of a red moon. Creatures from the dawning of this world shall rise and wreak havoc on the filth that has infested the earth. Seas will rage and swallow lands and when all have succumbed to her will, the age of darkness shall begin."

The phantom continued to look down at them both, Keela exhausted from his punishment. "Find and bring the amulet to Telloma. There you will unlock the power sealed beneath the mountain."

"Yes, my lord, as you command." Keela said submissively, bowing to the phantom. The pain kept him in the position as the phantom faded against the passing breeze.

Hours passed since his torture and now the second moon, Etai, had begun to rise over the horizon. Its bluish hue bathed the forest in a cold light with a campfire burning in front of him. Keela never liked the light, always preferring the comfort of darkness. For decades of his life, darkness and shadow had been his ally. Keela had lived his life in the wilderness ever since being abandoned by his parents when he was a child. His memories of the farm he grew up on were vague as were the faces of his parents, but one thing that permanently etched in his mind was the night his father and mother died. The sounds of his mother screaming as her father was brutalised by a gang of raiders that had come down from the mountains. Keela's father fought valiantly but ultimately died protecting his wife and son. His mother too died at the end of a spear leaving their son alone in the world. Keela had only survived because he had hidden under the floor of their hut. From that moment on Keela wandered the region alone and hungry, fighting for survival until one day coming across a cave to rest. Within that cave Keela found the one thing he thought he'd never have again, company. It had started off with nothing more than an echo in the darkness, a childlike giggle and as Keela explored the caves he found something he did not expect. Buried half in the dirt a stone, a jewel of deep purple with a streak of red at its centre. 'Hard to believe it had been seventy years since he found the spectre that tormented and tutored him', Keela thought. Since that day Keela had never been alone, always bound to darkness.

Tonight however, his ally felt absent. Lying next to him Ariel slept silently, the convulsing had ceased but the Phantom's violent assault now just a painful memory. A bit further away his companions laid sleeping silently as well. In the distance the burning lights of Artheria glowed in the night, the stars shining down upon them.
Ariel in a panic roused from her sleep. Frantically looking around her, the sight of Keela next to her calmed her a little.
"You were a fool to try and stop him." Keela said coldly. Ariel looked at him as he continued to stare out over the valley.
"Anymore and he would have killed you." She responded. Her eyes sparkled with the firelight, the first sign of life from her cold appearance. "You cannot serve if you are dead." The glimpse of caring extinguished from her voice. Keela remained focused on Artheria in the distance.
"He would not kill me." Keela muttered to himself. "I am a servant of Shassa, death is irrelevant.".
Doubt crept in her mind. "He was killing you, I stopped him."
"You cannot stop a god." Keela snapped. His voice remained quiet but had lost none of his authority. Ariel recoiled at the outburst. "We serve Nightshade and Shassa, and our lord has commanded us to find the amulet."
Ariel looked out over the calming vista ahead of them, she couldn't remember the last time they had slept indoors, eating and drinking till their fill. As much as that would be welcomed, she knew and believed in the sacrifice she

made to be with Keela. She hoped by completing their duty and resurrecting their goddess that her and Keela would finally be freed from their oath, to finally rest in peace together till the end of their days. The lingering doubt in her head pushed that joyous thought to the back of her head and she knew they had retrieved the amulet, and soon.

"What are your orders, my lord." Ariel jumped to her feet brushing off the debris from the forest floor. Keela's eyes remained fixed on the city ahead.

"We travel to the city in a few hours, I have an idea of where to start."

Two's Company
Chapter 14

Since the discovery and realisation of the amulet, Kyle had struggled to sleep at all. The power of Bellatris, the warrior queen, slayer of Nightshade and ruler of the northern realms, had been all he could think about. He and Felix had talked over supper about his journey ahead till the early hours of the morning before Felix retired to his bedroom. Although the muttering continued throughout their discussions, Kyle was still curious as to the changes in personality.

The sun had begun to creep in through the high windows above his head. It's warm orange glow bouncing off the bronzed crest that hung above the fireplace. Still tired, Kyle rose from a makeshift bed of blank parchment using his rucksack as a pillow. High above him curled in the corner of the rafters, Domina hung asleep for a couple hours, waking every now and then to check on her prize. There was no reason for her to leave, this was as good a place as any to sleep.

"Ah good morning." A voice shouted from above him. Looking around he saw Felix standing on a balcony above him. "I trust you slept well, can't have you falling asleep on your journey now can we." His manner had changed, different from the formal or aggressive. Felix seemed cheerful as he made his way down a spiral stone staircase. In his hands, a small basket filled with food and other supplies needed for a long journey.

"I did thank you." Kyle stuttered, still confused by the sudden manner of Felix.

"Good, the last thing we need you doing is falling asleep and waking up to a Naaba Dragon." Felix chuckled to himself. "Terrible gigantic creatures with its four fangs, and eyes. Did I ever tell you about the time I came upon a nest of them?" Felix's absent mindedness concerned Kyle. "Forgive me but may I ask you something?".
"Of course, what's on your mind?". Kyle took a second to find the words, as he carefully considered each one.
"You seem, different." Felix looked amused as Kyle collected the remainder of his thoughts.
"If you mean different, you are referring to my condition, I assure you I am completely fine." Felix chuckled again as Kyle faced show the awkwardness of his curiosity. Felix placed down the provisions onto the table. "As a young man such as yourself, I explored the hundreds and thousands of books, fascinated by what knowledge they might hold." Felix signalled for Kyle to pass his rucksack. "One day I came across a particular stone that I believed to be pure Mana that left me, well as you see me know." Kyle stood in silence as Felix's attitude to his past fell gravely on his face. "Wisdom was not a quality I possessed in my youth, something I hope you will learn quicker than I did." Felix smiled as he passed his rucksack back.

The early hours of the morning whittled on as Felix showed the safest route to Kyle. It passed many rivers and villages along its path north.
"When you reach the Fellarne river east of Mawold village there will be an ancient stone bridge further upstream, Unninas pass, it will be more discreet and quicker to Beltoria."
Kyle nodded as he digested the rush of information as he studied the map's route. The detail on the parchment amazed Kyle, every road and stream were drawn with such

detail, it was as if he was looking down on the world itself. For the next hour Kyle sat and had breakfast with Felix in the study. Satisfied she had heard enough of their plan, the rumble in Domina's stomach was enough of a signal to leave. Leaping silently between the beams with such grace until she reached the broken window she entered, she glanced down one more time. Felix smiled to himself as he glanced up to the broken window above them.

The sun finally had risen above the high walls of the city, its warming light was chilled by the cool morning sea breeze as it rolled off the harbour that was situated down the road. Kyle and Felix had parted ways outside the Bazaar. 'Keep it safe' were the last words Felix asked of Kyle. As Kyle walked through the streets of the city, for the first time in his life he felt alone. Thousands of people lived and worked in the city and each one was oblivious to the item he now protected. Little did he know that above him, Domina followed him across the rooftops. Careful not to let her shadow cast on the ground below she continued to watch from a distance. After a few minutes of wandering Kyle had managed to finally become lost in the labyrinth of streets. Asking a couple of people, Kyle managed to get back on course however his unfamiliarity of the street garnered attention from a suspicious looking group of young men. Following Kyle like a group of hungry dogs, they waited until Kyle had managed to end up lost in an alleyway. 'How do I even get out of this city! Never mind travel to Beltoria' Kyle wondered.
"What's up, you lost?" The lead man spoke, a false sincerity in his voice, "Come with me, I can help you find what you're looking for." The others started to spread out across the entrance to the alley. Kyle saw them slow

positioning themselves around the street. Kyle grew apprehensive.

"Thank you for the offer but I'm fine, I'm just leaving the city."

"Well I can show you the way, all we ask is for a little something for our service." Kyle saw straight through the man's false intentions. Kyle slowly reached for the grip on his sword.

"I have only a little food, and not enough to spare." The man smiled, his blackened teeth holding back the venom of his words.

"That's fine, because we weren't going to share. We were going to take everything." The group slowly closed in on Kyle. Seeing there was no escape, Kyle unsheathed his sword and bared it forward. The glistening blade forced a couple to stop in their tracks however the remaining either through courage or hunger continued to close in.

"I'm warning you, leave and I will not harm you." Kyle said mustering as much authority as he could. The men however saw through him, a couple even chuckled amongst themselves.

A passing shadow above them caused the group to look up. Blinded by the sun above, a shadow descended upon them with a fierce flurry. In the first few seconds Domina had landed on one of the gang members and sprung up to kick another along their flank. The confusion was enough for Domina to kick and punch the remaining three members to the ground. Kyle stood on in amazement at the fighting spectacle as Domina jumped, flipped and countered the returning attacks. Unprepared and bruised, the gang finally retreated from the alley as they dispersed into the crowds. Barely out of breath Domina turned to face Kyle who remained with his sword at the ready.

"You can put the sword down now. It's a dead giveaway you won't use it." She remarked as she swept a loose hair out of her face. Kyle looked at his blade for a moment before slowly returning it back into its sheath.

"I would have use it, I just don't want to kill anyone for the sake of it." Domina moved to sit down on a nearby basket.

"How do you know I wasn't..."

"Yeah, yeah I'm going to stop you right there. The blade is clean." Domina looked at Kyle with a patronising smile, "Anyone with a blade that clean is either a thief or coward, now since you don't like either, I'd say you've never fought anyone before." Kyle looked away in embarrassment at her accurate description of him. To alleviate the awkward silence Kyle began to walk towards the entrance to the alleyway.

"What you should be saying is thank you." Her remark sparked in his mind. Her actions did help him and pushing his pride aside Kyle turned to her and politely said "Thank you, now I must be on my way, the road is long, and I have wasted too much time already."

Domina leaped to her feet and quickly walked to catch up to him.

"So, where you headed? Anywhere interesting?" Domina asked remaining coy. Kyle continued to march towards the gates of the city. He glanced at her face; a feeling of trust came over him. Unsure whether it was her saving him or the attractiveness of her face, the first he noticed was her brown eyes.

"I'm heading north to Beltoria." Kyle responded. Domina's reaction to this already known news was seamless. Years of perfecting her skills played in her favour.

"Now that sounds like an adventure." Domina giggled. Kyle found her giggle cute as she smiled at him. "Well sounds like we're going to have some fun." Kyle stopped as he quickly realised what she had said.

"We?" he asked, confused by the jump in conversation.

"Yeah, come on like you've said we got a long way to go before nightfall." Kyle stuttered to find his words as Domina stopped a couple meters in front.

"We? But I didn't ask you to come along?" Kyle's confusion grew, "Why do you even want to come to Beltoria?" Domina walked towards him, flicking her hair back. "You look like you could use a friend, after the alleyway, who could blame you for someone having your back." Domina put her arm around his shoulders as she started to push him front towards the gates, "I've seen this city, now it's time to explore somewhere else. I've seen the road to Beltoria, a lot of dangerous places, people and things out there in the wilderness." Domina came to a stop in front of Kyle. "You ever come across a Naaba Dragon or a Darabu Wilderbeast? Trust me, you need someone like me watching your back." The seriousness in her voice broke as she smiled at him again. "Besides, nothing wrong with having company on a journey like this." She patted Kyle's shoulder and made way towards the gates. 'She does make a point.' Kyle thought as he watched her walk calmly away. Unsure about the road ahead he set off following her.

Three hours had passed by the time they had finally cleared the farming fields north of the city. As Kyle reached the summit of a small mound, he looked back over the golden wheat that waved in the calm breeze. Farms were nothing new to him, but the sheer expanse of farmland that supplied the city was incredible. The noises of the cramp city now but a memory and only the sounds of nature surrounded him. Coming up immediately behind him Domina looked at him, his amazed by his wonder of the world. For many years she had travelled places, seen great and captivating things, but as the years went by the world seemed smaller to her.

"What, you never seen a field of wheat before, farm-boy?" She asked with a smirk on her face as she passed him.

"Yes, of course." Kyle replied as he glanced once more at the magnificent view before descending the hill. "I'm not a farmer, I worked on a boat."

Kyle thoughts immediately ran to his father. Usually, he would be working on the sea or fixing the nets by now. Since the attack the worry of if his family even survived made him uneasy.

"Well you're still a country boy and not even a local one at that." Domina glanced momentarily back to study the look on Kyle's face. Like gambling Domina knew everything can be read on a person's face. All you needed was a little practice, to which she had plenty.

"Why are you travelling so far on your own then?" She enquired hoping to fish for more information. The sudden barrage of truth and questions unsettled Kyle.

"How do you know I'm not from around here?" Domina came to a stop, a smug smile appeared in the corner of her lips.

"First thing is your face." Kyle was surprised by the remark, "Everything you see is like you're seeing it for the first time."

Words escaped Kyle as he tried to respond, he was amazed by her insight and concerned by her accuracy. Domina could see Kyle begin to recoil from the conversation, her fishing was at risk.

"Come on we got a long way to travel before nightfall. I know a place over the next hill." Domina whipped around and began to walk around a small stream.

The rest of the afternoon was without event. For miles the journeyed north crossing great plains of grassland. Dotted around the plains, wilder beast roamed in herds as they grazed. Far into the west thunder showers rained down, the dull grey clouds frenzied with lightning. As they clambered up the hillside amongst the trees, the setting sun pierced through the branches. In the breaks of the trees Kyle saw the rising of Tlao, the largest moon. Its body took up most of the horizon in the south a usual sight as summer gave way to autumn. One of the many stories Kyle had been read to as a child was of Tlao and Etai the lovers. His mother had told him the story of two lovers who defied the will of their god and as punishment, they were lifted to the heavens to forever chase each other. Kyle had always thought the story was sad, but his mother reminded him that every so often the two moons would eclipse each other, allowing the lovers to embrace for a night.

Upon High
Chapter 15

With the last light of the sun fading behind the horizon Kyle and Domina had to rely on the moonlight and aurora to guide them. Tlao was already high above the horizon which meant Etai, the smaller of the two moons was close behind. Although it had been a good day's walk from the outskirts of Artheria, the journey so far had been uneventful. Kyle still couldn't shake this feeling that the Blades might be close behind, ready to strike the moment it was right. Kyle every now and then made sure to check behind them.

"You alright?"

Kyle quickly turned to see Domina a little further ahead up the hill. His newfound guide was the latest in a long line of mysteries that he could only hope to try to understand. For the most part she seemed to be exactly who she said she was, even suggesting cutting through the great Telloma forest to avoid bandits that might prey on them on the main road.

"Yeah, just admiring the view?" Kyle replied, trying his best to hide his suspicions. Domina held her gaze for a moment before turning to point a little further up the hill.

"Not far, just beyond the cliffside, we can rest then."

Walking along the cliffside alarmed Kyle as he looked over the edge to the sharp drop below. The cove was so deep, Kyle imagined the maw of a giant beast ready to devour him, the razor-sharp rocks like teeth. A slight gust of wind rushed past Kyle causing him to press harder against the cliff face. Domina instead leaped from stone to stone without a thought or care of the drop below. At any other time, Kyle might have admired her agility, but the long drop below consumed most of his courage. Step by step he slowly crossed the ravine, his heart pounding so fast, if the fall didn't kill him, his heart just might.

Finally, they reached the other side of the cove and Kyle prayed to whoever would listen that he was thankful to be back on solid ground. Resting against a tree, Domina watched as Kyle panted and took a moment to recover. His heart slowed down enough but the sound of chuckling caused him to look up.

"What's so funny?" Kyle shot as he slowly got to his knee.

"You. Thought you'd be up for a little adventure."

Before Kyle could answer back, he noticed something hidden amongst the trees and grass. His eyes adjusted more to the low light, but he could just make out huge carved stones. A ruin.

Its once proud and huge frame had been swallowed by the centuries of overgrowth now reclaimed, the land leaving only a shred of its former glory. Giant stone blocks made up its outer wall, the vines wrapped firmly around the columns of the entrance.

"What is this place?" Kyle asked, his eyes wide. The path leading up to the entrance was overgrown like the building, only the odd stone still on show. Domina came to a stop just inside the ruin to see Kyle lent against a wall.

"Don't know, some old ruin, found when I was travelling from Beltoria." Kyle could see she had little interest in ever knowing what its past was. Glancing round he started to think of the possibilities, enough so that even in his tired state Kyle began to wander. Eight weathered cravings lined one wall nearby each tucked into an alcove on what was once a corridor leading away from the entrance. Curious about the place, Kyle pushed further into the ruin.

Stones and shattered tiles littered the ground, grass now growing over them. Each footstep Kyle made disturbed them with a crack. In the centre of the ruin, a half standing keep remained defiant against the elements, its roof had caved in which exposed the wooden beams. Everything inside had rotted away leaving just the remnants of the multiple floors. Etched into the archway above a collapsed doorway an ancient symbol similar to the writing in Felix's old tomes. Kyle marvelled at the realisation of the ruin; it was the stronghold of Baradis. Kyle remembered back to his time reading at the monastery and the battles of the Dawning war. Baradis, the ancient fort that Arturus and Bellatris made their plans before Fellarne river. The feeling of history flew through him like a breeze as he imagined the sights on that day, the soldiers preparing for battle, fires and forges burning. As he wandered further down the corridor Kyle came to an opening. The large room was open to the world, looking out over the valley below and its centre a granite table. The roof had long since fallen in on the room however still sections remained intact. Rusted sconces littered the walls and withered torches lay in them.

Kyle stood for a few minutes soaking in the significance of the place, his fantasy had come to life. As he looked out over the valley, the aurora flowed in the heavens. It's slow change from greens to purples was as stimulating and wondrous as anything in the world. His solitude of silence was broken by the sudden sharp breeze.

"Hello Kyle." A voice called from behind. The soft-spoken voice caused him to turn without hesitation. Standing in front of him a beautiful woman, the same from his dream. Her face was as pale and pure as snow, her flowing brown hair lined with flowers and crowned.

"Who are you?" Kyle asked, his words struggled to come out. The woman smiled softly as she approached.

"I am the mother." She smiled.

"I saw you in my dream, but I don't recognise you." The woman continued to smile as she reached the edge of the floor, the dark maw far below.

"Yes, but you have heard my voice on the wind." Her gentle voice reminded him of his mother. Every worry and doubt in his mind had vanished. He felt her as if she could see through him to his very soul. "Do not be afraid my child, you will face many challenges on the path ahead." Kyle began to think about the discussion with Felix, the looming thought of Nightshade returning sparked fear in his mind. 'I hope I have the courage,' Kyle thought.

"Courage comes from fear, in time you will find yours." The woman spoke as she looked out over the valley. Kyle stood shocked as if she heard his thoughts.

"Who are you, my lady?" Kyle politely asked, "How do you know what I'm thinking?"

"I see the doubt in your eyes for they are the troubles in my heart." Kyle looked at her confused at the riddles she spoke. "I am the mother of all things, the trees, the flowers and beasts. My body is the earth, my voice is the wind, my eyes shine like the stars."

A sudden thought hit him like a charging Ox.

"You're Idella?" Kyle exclaimed, his jaw hanging open. Idella smiled and nodded gently. He fell to his knees, so many emotions overwhelmed him. As he tried to process the situation in his mind, a gentile hand extended towards him.

"Rise, you have no need to bow." Kyle looked up at the glowing face of his god, the mother of all beings, "You have many questions child, but there is little time to answer so many."

Kyle clambered to his feet, "You spoke to me in my dream, the world on fire and people I've never seen?"

"These are things that could come to pass should the Shadow Blades take the amulet."

The reality of his quest broke through the feeling of serenity, replacing it with dread. Doubt and fear crept into his eyes.

"Why don't you take the amulet, you're a god, you could take it far away."

"I cannot take the amulet." Idella shook her head, "The same way you could not take a stone from the Endless Gardens. The amulet cannot be taken from this place, it is bound to this plain of existence, as is its prisoner."

"What about Shassa, you could defeat her?" Kyle panicked.

"No more than you could defeat a part of yourself. There are things beyond this realm that you would not believe, in the Void we are all one, but many. Shassa does not come from the Void, *it* is from somewhere else entirely."

"If she, it, wants to destroy the world, how is she different from Yema?"

Idella moved away from the window towards a withered tree branch.

"Life is made through balance, Yema like all the gods create that balance." Idella reached out to the dead branch and with a touch, life filled the limb. Buds sprouted from it into blooming flowers. "Even in death there is always life, Shassa seeks to take all life."

Kyle looked out at the world, the starlight and moons shining down like guardians. He pulled out the amulet from his rucksack and held it in his hand.

"How can I hope to defeat Shassa or her followers?" He muttered, the doubt filling his voice.

"You will not be alone." Kyle turned around to see Idella looking down on him, "You will face the dangers ahead with many allies, all of whom will come to believe in you." The pressure of the task ahead began to weigh heavier in his mind. "They will help you carry this burden, I have seen it."

"What else have you seen?" Kyle pleaded, hoping for good news.

"That your journey will take you home." Idella spoke softly as she stepped away. A gentle breeze blew across her and like leaves on the wind she faded from sight. Silence fell on the ruin again and Kyle felt more alone now than ever before. He realised his family wherever they were, must be half a world away.

Taking one last look around the room, Kyle tried to shift his mind back to the heroes of old, standing on the eve of battle, not knowing how it would play out. Without a sound Domina rounded the corner to see a conflicted Kyle. "There you are, have a good look round?" Domina chuckled. Kyle forced out a smile. "Amazing view though, right?" Kyle nodded silently again. Feeling he was hiding something, Domina watched him intently. From her experiences everyone had a tell and Kyle was like reading a flag, easy to spot. Looking around the room in approval Domina took a step towards the granite table. "Looks like as good a place as any to camp, even a bed." Domina grinned knocking on the table. Kyle's morbid attitude started to wear down on Domina.

"What's up with you? You look as if the world is crushing you."

"It's nothing," Kyle spoke softly as he placed his rucksack on the floor. "I just miss my family is all."

Domina jumped up onto the table and sat, her sword clanging on the hard surface. She began to briefly adjust her attire until she felt comfortable.

"Where are they?" She asked.

"A little town called Rheia." Kyle responded as he slumped against the stone wall. "I left them when they needed me most, now I'm not sure if they're ok."

Domina tried to act as sincerely as possible but found it difficult. For as long as she could remember she had been abandoned, never having a home or a family to call her own. Throughout the years her sadness hardened and turned to anger before she used it to her advantage as she did most things.

"Sounds tough, to leave them all behind. You must be really doing something important?" Domina chose her words carefully determined to get more information out of him. The words struck Kyle to full effect as he tried to understand his journey. Domina began to change her attitude as she slid off the table and onto the floor.

"What's so important that you have to leave your family to go to Beltoria? I gotta tell you Beltoria isn't exactly a nice place if you come from the south."

Kyle looked at her inquisitively. "What do you mean?"

"Well for starters the north is cold and dull, the city is massive and built of dark stone. Not the friendliest of places."

"Where are you from?" Kyle asked. The question was one Domina had practiced many a time at lying about but the vulnerability and innocence of Kyle made her speak easier.

"I'm from a place out west as far west as you can go called Shanktown." Kyle was taken aback by the name. "Don't worry it's a nickname more than anything. It is a bit of a weird place, but the people are from all over the world trading anything. I've even got a few friends there still."

Domina smiled as she laid down on the ground under the stone table. "Play your cards right, I might take you there." She closed her eyes leaving Kyle to mull over the seed she just planted.

Written Among the Stars
Chapter 16

The incandescent aurora flowed across a snowy sky, shades of green streaking between the clouds. The monochromatic landscape occasionally drenched in colour in the breaks. It was an autumn evening and snow had been falling for a week covering everything in an ice-cold blanket. Nestled in the woods was a clearing with a cosy farm at its centre. All the animals had been herded into the barn leaving the fields to rest in its snowy slumber.

An elderly woman staggered through the trees, branches and twigs snapped under her footsteps. She was cold and shivering in the freezing temperatures. Annabelle fell to her knees as she felt a striking pain across her body. Dressed in what seemed to once be a noble outfit, now torn and dirtied by her travels in the wilderness. Looking around her, she felt as if she had finally fallen into her grave waiting to be buried. In the distance she saw a faint light flicker. 'Finally, my mind is playing tricks' she thought as the light continued to beckon her, 'Still, could be better than laying here to die.' With what remaining strength she had, Annabelle made her way towards the light. After a few minutes of stumbling through the trees Annabelle finally came into a clearing. Seeing the farm just a short distance away, the flickering light became ever more inviting. Finally reaching the door, Annabelle heard a couple voices speaking to each other. Wrapping hard against the sturdy door, the voices stopped immediately and after a moment the door opened with a stiff creek.

"Please" Annabelle croaked, "Help me." Falling forward in exhaustion, she was caught by a strapping young man. Within a few seconds the room faded to black.

After a few hours, Annabelle had woken to the sound of burning logs, the smell of food cooking above the flames. Opening her eyes, a young couple sat staring at her.
"My lady, how are you feeling?" The woman asked curtsying as best she could. Annabelle looked around the room, unsure of how she ended up there. The room was low and made of bare wood and stone. Its furnishings were simple and handmade. "My lady?" The woman asked again.
"Grateful. I thought I may have finally met my end out there in the woods." Although she was now warm, Annabelle felt a great pain across her body. For weeks it had gotten worse, with only the cold to distract her from it.
"My name is Heidia and this is my husband Bain." Bain bowed his head as he was introduced. Annabelle acknowledged him as she sat up. The aroma of the food pulled her gaze from the couple. Heidia spotted and quickly served her a broth.
"Forgive me my lady, this is all we have." Heidia apologized, passing the simple bowl to her.
"There is no need to forgive," Annabelle dismissed, grabbing the bowl and began to eat the food, "it is more than I have had in some time."
Bain looked sceptical at Annabelle, "How did you end up all the way out here my lady, you are far from Tyne?"

Annabelle spent the rest of the evening regaling them with her ordeal and how she came about being in the forest.

Both listened on in amazement before finally ending in confusion.

"I'm sorry I may have misunderstood you, who exactly are you?" Bain asked, a force in his voice.

"I am Lady Annabelle of Tyne, Daughter of Lord Dravos and Lady Lara."

Annabelle was still not used to introducing herself to people. Growing up in such high stature servants would always announce her whenever she entered a room when a function was on. The couple continued to look confused at the name as they glanced at each other.

"My lady, lady Annabelle of Tyne is a young girl, no older than fifteen, you couldn't possibly be her." Heidia declared.

"I am Lady Annabelle." Annabelle said as she tried to raise her voice.

"If you are Lady Annabelle, why are you an old lady?" Bain responded, his calm demeanour slowly giving out to his confusion. "Besides the Lord and Lady of Tyne are dead, murdered," Annabelle fell silent at the words. Looking down at her hands, her skin withered and wrinkled. Shock spread across her as she moved to a basin of water, "Lady Annabelle has been missing for days." Annabelle looked into the basin to see an aged face staring back at her. Her hair was grey, eyes milky and skin sagging. Feelings of confusion and pain started to overwhelm her as she tried to comprehend the situation. Her heart began to race to the point she could feel it trying desperately to escape. 'How is this possible?' Annabelle thought as she continued to stare at every inch of her, 'could this be a nightmare, magic?'

"The Lord and Lady were said to be murdered with a knife." Annabelle heard the words and reached for the knife on her waist. It wasn't there.

Thud.

Annabelle turned around to see the knife glinting in the firelight. It's dragon hilt sparkled, and a sudden urge came over Annabelle as if it called to her.

"This is a kingly gift, my lady." Bain slowly stood up. His hospitality now gone and replaced with hostility, "How did you come by it?"

Annabelle tried hard to concentrate on what Bain was asking but all of her focus was on the knife, an urge of some kind calling out to her.

"It was a gift." Annabelle muttered.

"I don't believe you or your story. An old lady couldn't have survived out there and now you claim to be Lady Annabelle." Bain ushered for Heidia to step back.

"I think you are the one that killed the Lord and Lady." Bain reached for a sword that hung from a crossbeam nearby.

"You are right." Annabelle muttered again, the frightened tone in her voice all but turned to a sinister one.

She finally gave into the instincts and dashed for the knife with almost unnatural speed. In a quick motion Annabelle unsheathed the knife and sliced Bain's throat. Heidia let out a high-pitched scream as Bain fell to his knees grasping at his throat. As Heidia turned to run, Annabelle grabbed her by the arm and swung her round. The knife plunged into her chest with ease. A rush of ecstasy filled Annabelle as agonising pain flowed through Heidia. With every passing second the life from Heidia drained and Annabelle felt invigorated. After a minute a husk of the beautiful Heidia fell to the floor in front of Bain.

"I *am* the one that killed the lord and lady." Annabelle continued; confidence poured from her voice. She turned around to Bain to reveal a younger beautiful woman her pale skin, tight and glowing, her hair now flowing white.

Bain tried to speak but to no avail. Without a second thought Annabelle stepped forward and plunged the knife into Bain's chest. The ecstasy rushed through her again as all the life drained from him until nothing more than bone remained. The farm stood silent as Annabelle relished in the last moments of pleasure, her hunger satisfied. The slow sound of clapping broke the silence. Annabelle whipped round to see Keela standing in the open doorway.

"Excellent." He said, a smile on his face.

"What have you done to me?" Annabelle shouted her grip on the knife now tighter than ever.

"I have given you what you wanted," Keela said as he strolled towards her, "Freedom. Freedom from your parents, freedom from being married to someone you despised, to be bought and bartered like livestock. I gave you *everything* you wanted." Keela came to a stop in front of her, the knife pressed against his chest.

"You abandoned me, you made me into a monster." Annabelle could feel the emotions beginning to overflow. Tears started to well in her eyes as her mind played out the murders of her parents, of the young couple.

"I gave you everything you wanted, like anything, you have to pay a small price for greatness." Annabelle looked up at Keela, his eyes filled with confidence and adoration. "You are amazing, to become so much more than you were. Together we can do so much more." Keela placed his hand on the blade. Annabelle resisted as he pressed lightly against the blade.

She remembered the night she first met him; a dashing young man filled with confidence. He had come to be an advisor to her father. The moment she met him there was something about him that stood out from the many men her father had introduced to her. Every one of them was the same as the last, grown from money, believing it to be everything, but Keela's confidence, his mind had come from something else. For weeks they had met in secret at night just outside the grounds of her father's estate. At first, they spoke of many things that enthralled her and opened her eyes to things beyond her small world. As they continued to meet, speaking became passion, until the night he visited Annabelle in her room. They had spoken of running away together, travelling the world, but she was scared her father would track her down and drag her back to her cage. Keela had presented her with an escape and a pledge to give her anything she desired, in return she had to do the same. The knife in his hand was exquisitely made, shining and captivating to her, she even thought it was calling her from the moment her eyes laid upon it. That night she crept into her parent's chambers and plunged the knife into her father's chest. Within seconds her body pulsed as he screamed out. The intensity grew but she couldn't release her grip on the blade. A great pain felt as if she was being torn in two but at the same time a great pleasure washed over her. Her mother screamed all the while until in an act of overwhelming emotions, Annabelle thrust the blade into her mother. In one night, she had destroyed her world to make way for a new future.

Reaching where she and Keela had planned to meet she could hear the alarms of the castle ring out. Men shouted as they ran about the castle walls and surrounding village. She was desperate to escape but Keela was nowhere to be found. He had abandoned her, ruined her life, until now.

His presence calmed her as the blade slowly lowered until finally resting at her side. He had been true to his word and given her everything she wanted, just not as she imagined. Keela gently kissed her on the forehead and looked into her eyes again.

"He was right about one thing."

"What was that?" Annabelle asked. Keela turned and walked towards the door with purpose.

"You are no longer Lady Annabelle." Annabelle followed him into the cold night. As she stepped through the threshold, the bite of the evening chill was nowhere to be felt. Keela looked up to the aurora that had broken through the clouds. Annabelle saw beyond the amazement of the colours to the stars above. The world shone in brilliant vibrance, far flung from earlier. A group of stars stood out to her more than the overs, an old constellation that she loved from her childhood.

"Ariel." Annabelle spoke to herself.

A Monument to All Our Sins
Chapter 17

High above Artheria, the stars shone down gently, their light masked by the aurora that bathed the world in colour light. Ariel gazed at them, thinking back to the last time she had that fateful night. Her thoughts kept wandering to the past decades. She had largely forgotten the majority of the countless people that kept her hunger at bay, so she could serve. At first it was to keep her from the guilt of her actions but as time moved on, so did her remorse. Fear gave way to love, guilt to joyous ecstasy. Tonight though, the hunger had returned. It had been nearly a week and already she could feel the aching setting in.

Hidden amongst the shadows of a doorway, her eyes were the only sign of life from within the darkness that she found so comforting. The streets had died down to the odd drunk, nightwalker and seedy individuals that preferred the night as much as her. Just down the street a tavern full of life and, to Ariel, the possibility of peace. The idea of going into the building was of little interest to her. Ariel was repulsed as she remembered the sights and sounds of when she first started using taverns as her release. Every sense was on fire and overwhelmed, the smell of vomit, sweat and unsavoury food made her sick to her stomach. Even the people she fed on had a less than appealing taste. After those experiences, Ariel retreated to the solitude of the night to find her victims.

Whether it was fate or the goddess of death herself it didn't take long for a worthy feast to show themselves. That feast took the form of a drunk man and woman as they stumbled out of the tavern doorway. Ariel grinned a sick smile at the irony of a couple of this night of all nights. The unsuspecting couple made their way along the street merrily chatting and flirting with each other. As they passed, Ariel recognised her as a bar wench, the man a paying customer. 'Perfect' Ariel thought as they went down a nearby alley. Checking the street one last time Ariel lifted her mask up and sprung from the shadows darting across the street to the alleyway. Her hunger would be satisfied soon enough.

A scream rang out momentarily before being cut short. Keela looked over at his shoulder to the broken window with a sadistic smile. Scattered about the room, the Blades searched through piles of books and scrolls. Felix's empire of books had been ransacked and thrown about the room. "As I was saying, we are here to reclaim something that was not yours to begin with *Knight*." Keela spoke the words soaking with malice. Felix was bound to his chair, cuts and bruises covered his face and body. "Now for most people physical pain is enough to loosen their tongues, but you know, and I know, you are not a normal person, are you?" Keela stood over him in utter domination.
"I've heard the stories about a scholar in Artheria who is believed to be crazy, who collects lost artefacts of Cyrilla, who believes the city still exists." Keela looks around at the mass of relics and other objects. One particular object caught his attention, the statue. "I find that it is often the crazed individual that was right all along." Standing before it, Keela studied the features on the face intently. "I can see you haven't quite lost all of your looks have you, since we last spoke."
"I would remember a vagabond like you." Felix responded. A sudden shift in his attitude, "Get out thieves or I'll send

you straight to the abyss." He spat. Keela calmly watched on as Felix battled his personalities inside.

"A nasty condition you have, Master." Keela spoke softly. He slithered back to Felix and sat down opposite him, his eyes fixed. "It looks familiar to a condition a scholar wrote about some time ago, a side-effect if I'm not mistaken." Felix sat silently as Keela hissed. Keela glanced back to the glowing stone in the statue's hand. Felix glanced too before meeting Keela's eyes once more. "It said that this person tried to pass his essence onto another body." Keela smiled. "Being able to remember everything from one's past can be a dangerous thing Felix. Sometimes they can come back to haunt you." Keela stared at him intently as Felix saw past the scars and hatred in his eyes. A flash of a memory clicked in his mind.

"Keela?" Felix realised.

"All these years and you are still as pathetic as the day I met you." Keela sneered.

"I remember a bright young lad. In all those years I still regret not seeing you for what you are." All the memories of Keela flooded back to him.

"Powerful? Intelligent?"

"A pawn. A slave to the darkness inside you." Keela kicked back his chair in rage. The force knocked over towers of books drawing the attention of his blades.

"I am no-one's pawn old man!" Keela shouted, his face trembling in rage, "In the centuries you've lived you've had power at your finger-tips but were too afraid to use it." Looking at his Blades who stood silently watching Keela charge the Mana in his hands. "Now I have power, when I retrieve the amulet, I will unleash Nightshade and be gifted power beyond measure." In his rage Keela unleashed his energy at the bronze statue. The energy impacted on it instantly melting the metal and shattering it to the floor.

"Now I'm going to make the last few moments of your long and dull life incredibly painful." Keela removed his coat to show the extent of the scarring on his arms. His skin looked to have been stitched back together by himself. Felix looked on, the violence of his life as clear on his skin as the hatred in his eyes. Keela darted to within a few inches of Felix's face. As he came to a stop his true master emerged from his body. The shadow formed around half of Keela's and hissed.

"Tell me where the child has gone."

"I do have one more regret." Felix spoke softly, his calm personality on display. Keela looked at him with malice. "I regret not helping a young man when he asked me for help." Felix grew tired from the night as he rested his head on the back of his reading chair. The heat from the fire felt cosy on him.

"For that I am sorry." Without any regret or second thought Keela placed his hand on Felix's head and the surge of Mana between the two whipped and cracked.

For hours Keela tortured Felix, tearing through his mind and memories until he found what he was looking for, the location of Kyle. Exhausted from the ordeal, Keela recomposed himself and turned to address his followers. "The boy is heading to Beltoria. I want you all to go to every city, town, village and farm between here and Beltoria to find him." All of the Blades left the room quickly and marched out of the house leaving Ariel and Keela alone. Keela's breathing laboured as he lent against the table. Ariel had been the only one to see Keela in such a vulnerable position. There had only been a few times he had ever shown weakness in front of her, but he trusted her implicitly.

"There was someone else in the room when that boy was here, a girl you are familiar with." Keela looked at her. Ariel instantly thought of one person who had come across her and survived. "I want you to find her and get her and get that amulet.". Ariel nodded.

"I know where I can find her."

The Road Less Travelled
Chapter 18

The morning had been of little interest as Kyle and Domina set out from the ruin to scale further into the mountains. The morning sun had slowly given way to the looming black clouds from the north. Their dark towering columns that reached to the heavens had Kyle foreboding the coming days. Domina however had dismissed them at a second glance as she pushed further up the hill. For an hour their assent had changed from a walk into a march by the time the midday sun was in the sky.

"Can we stop for a moment, I need to rest." Kyle asked panting. Domina came to a halt on a ridgeline. She looked back down to see Kyle sitting on a boulder.

"What's the hold up, we're nearly there." Domina said, pointing to a way up the hill. In the distance they could both hear the faint roar of the Fellarne river. "We need to cross and be heading down by nightfall. You don't want to be caught up here when those clouds hit." Domina knew the consequences of being on the mountain when a storm hit. In her travels many talked about people missing or falling to their deaths during storms. She had dismissed their warnings until she herself made the mistake of being caught up the mountain. For two days she huddled under a boulder as lightning lashed down on the mountainside. The roaring of thunder and river was so loud she struggled to sleep. Only on the third day she left the safety of her hole to see the flooding had swept away trees and rocks. "The bridge is only a few hundred metres up the hill." Hearing the faint river and looking at the never-ending ridgeline, Kyle mustered himself to his feet and began to climb the hill once more.

The path had finally levelled out to the joy of Kyle who now battled the aches in his legs. He had never climbed so much in his life and after looking down the valley, felt it was enough for a lifetime. Snaking through the trees a path had been carved out as Kyle saw stones lay under the dirt.

"Up ahead." Domina pointed as they both quickened their pace to see the rise of the bridge. It's light-coloured stones, similar to that of the ruin they slept in, made it stand out amongst the trees. As they reached the edge they came to an immediate stop.

The bridge was gone.

All that remained of the ancient bridge were piles of rubble and stone on either side of the gorge, the river roaring down in the middle. All excitement evaporated from Kyle's body as he slumped down on the rubble. Domina scanned the debris of the bridge.

"It must have been the river during the last storm." She said turning around to see a defeated Kyle. His mood poured from him as he stared into space. "It's not a problem, we just got to the next crossing."

"You don't understand, I need to get to Beltoria as soon as possible." Kyle snapped as he continued to look ahead of him. "There must be some way across the river."

"The bridge is gone." Domina snapped back. "What's the rush? Why do you need to get there so fast?" Kyle hesitated for a moment at the question, he knew she had been pushing to know for some time but had managed to resist.

"I need to deliver something quickly."

"What? What is so important that you would risk crossing here!" Kyle tried his best to avoid eye contact with her as she stared at him. Domina had been in his company for the best part of week and in that time, she helped him bear the burden of his quest without so much as a wonder why. With the seriousness of his quest and the importance of the amulet, Kyle remembered his conversation with Idella. 'Maybe she would one of the people Idella mentioned' Kyle debated, as he mulled over whether to show her or not. Silently Kyle opened his bag and pulled out the amulet. The golden relic shimmered brightly in the daylight. Domina's eyes widened at her prize.

"This is why I need to get to Beltoria quickly. It's the reason why I had to leave my village."

Domina slowly approached the amulet like a magpie, unable to resist the valuable object.

"Is it dangerous?" She asked as she raised her hand to it.

"Yes and so are the people after it."

Domina stopped dead and looked at him. Although she had heard the story back in Artheria, she allowed him to tell his tale to her in more detail. With the prize so close to her, she knew that it was an item worth taking.

"So you are being hunted by Shadow Blades?"

Kyle nodded. Domina stood up immediately and stood back."Well, it's nice to have met you, but this is where I leave you." Domina spoke as fearfully as possible. Her gamble had begun. Whilst it was mostly a ploy of hers, Domina had herself been unfortunate to cross a shadow blade in the past. The encounter had nearly cost her life, but she managed to slip away.

Confused by the sudden change in attitude Kyle watched as Domina started to walk away.

"Where are you going?" Kyle asked as she continued to walk away.

"Leaving you, I didn't sign up to be hunted by Blades."

Domina slowed her pace to allow Kyle to catch up.

"I need your help. I can't do this on my own and you managed to stop those guys back in the city."
Domina swung herself round to face Kyle.
"Look there is a *huge* difference between thugs and Blades. I've heard of Blades before and what they can do and trust me, that's not worth my time." Domina continued to play her choreographed dance of lies and fear. Kyle saw a glint in her eyes as she spoke. He desperately thought of anything to make her stay until one word rang out in his mind.
"How much?" Kyle asked, his desperation turning to curiosity. Domina stopped and looked at him. "How much for you to help?"
For most of Domina's life, haggling and bartering had become the only way to make a living and survive. The rules she made as a child had kept her alive, for that they were golden. First rule of bargaining, reject the first offer.
"It's not a question of how much, you know why no one tells stories about Shadow Blades?". Kyle shook his head.
"Because no one is ever alive after meeting one."
"I did." Kyle said with confidence.
"No you didn't, you could barely defend yourself in the city." Domina could sense his desperation. Her dance of deception now had competition.
"I did, during the village attack some of them chased me into the forest and attacked me."
Domina stood unconvinced.
"You mean to tell me, you, someone who barely knows how to hold a sword, fought Shadow Blades and won?"
Domina shook her head and turned. "I don't believe you."
Frustration built quickly in his mind. "I did." Kyle shouted as a sudden burst of energy released from his hands and the ground in front of Domina cracked. Domina jumped back in amazement. The ground continued to crack a little

more as she whipped round to see him standing with energy flowing around his hands. The look on Kyles's face told a similar story as he looked amazed at the sight. 'This could be more difficult than I thought' Domina thought. She had very rarely seen a Mana-Borne or even dealt with one.

Using her shock, she regrouped and quickly formed another plan in her mind.

"Why the hell didn't you tell me you were Mana-Borne?!" Kyle knew he had her attention by the look of shock on her face. Stunned himself that he was able to keep the power flowing he concentrated on keeping it together.

"I didn't want to scare you away, you've helped me so much already, I enjoyed having you around." A sincerity in his voice caused Domina to feel something. She always felt uneasy whenever her own feelings decided to interfere with her work. Although he had been moody and gullible at times, having someone around was a nice change from her usual activities.

"It's going to cost you." Domina spoke softly, her hard-exterior easing.

"Name your price?" Kyle asked. 'Finally, some good news' he thought as Domina mulled over the question.

"Gold and what else you got?" Domina asked, eyeing up the sword.

"It's not for sale." Kyle quacking responded clenching the pommel. "Once we get to Beltoria you'll be paid for your services, agreed?"

Domina took her time thinking over the terms. Gold for taking him to Beltoria wasn't such a bad prize but the prize could be so much more.

"Agreed."

Kyle held out his hand. Nodding she grasped his and they shook. 'Now to change the plan' Domina continued to think of a new idea. "So now we're agreed do you even know who you're supposed to meet in Beltoria?"

"I was told to meet a scholar called Razar in the Court district. He would take the amulet to the king of Beltoria." Domina knew that wouldn't work for her as she shook her head. Kyle looked at her reaction.

"Who's to say this Razar isn't working for the Blades? Or would sell it the second you leave it with him?"

"Felix told me that he has worked with him in the past." Domina continued to sow the seeds of doubt in his mind. "Cyrillian artefacts are extremely rare, and valuable, who's to say he hasn't been selling them on to someone else?" She could see the seeds beginning to sprout already. "It's still going to take us a week to get to Beltoria from here." Kyle started to question his plan. If the artefact was as priceless as Felix suggested, Kyle couldn't risk it falling into anyone's hands.

"I know a contact in Shanktown that deals with scholars and artefacts, maybe he could help find someone who could keep it safe?" Kyle couldn't believe the suggestion. Shanktown was the furthest place from Beltoria as possible.

"But that is in the wrong direction?".

Domina could feel she was so close to finishing her plan. "I know people there, I trust them, and you should trust me." Domina said with a smile. Kyle knew she was right, she had helped so far and if her reaction to the amulet was anything to say then she was as concerned as he was.

"How long will it take to get to Shanktown?" Kyle asked, still feeling nervous about the drastic change.

"Five days, six if the weather is bad, but if we follow the river down it'll take us to Clowetta, from there we can ride to Shanktown."

Kyle knew the Blades must be following hunting them, even up this mountain. A change in direction could help him buy some time to get the amulet to safety.

Into Darkness
Chapter 19

After thinking about the idea Kyle finally agreed and they
set off down the mountain. For hours they descended
beside the great river. Twice the river fell into a great
waterfall, falling hundreds of metres below into emerald
pools of glacial water. The alpine setting was peaceful with
the sounds of wildlife calling to each other. Every now and
then Kyle had forgotten the burden put on him or even the
fear of his pursuers. By mid-afternoon the sun was already
at beginning to set. Both tired from the trek up and
subsequently back down the mountain they agreed to rest
by one of the waterfalls. Despite its size the roar of the
water was rather quiet Kyle thought, setting his bag down
against one of the larger boulders by the water.

Kyle sat contemplating their change in direction as Domina
filled her container with water. He realised that after the
time they had spent together already he didn't know much
about her. 'Someone as well travelled and charismatic
must have some stories to tell' he thought as she finished
clinging to the side of a rock to catch the water.
"Where else have you been?" Kyle asked. Domina looked
back in confusion at the sudden question.
"What?"
"You say you've travelled the world, I'm just curious as to
where you've been?" He clarified. "You must have seen a
lot already."
Being asked questions was always a risky subject and her
mind had grown accustomed to deflecting any that came
her way.

"Why the sudden interest?" she replied. Kyle could feel a little defence in her voice.

"I just wanted to know more about you. If we're travelling together some stories could help pass the time."

This was indeed risky territory for Domina. She had made the mistake in the past of telling any truth of herself to someone before and she had paid a hefty price for it. Luckily, she had learnt from her past.

"I've been to a little island called Atana."

Kyle had heard of the name but little else. Many of the books he read weren't from outside the lands beyond Laxos.

"What's it like, I've never heard of it."

Domina sat down opposite him and took a bite of her meal.

"It's a beautiful place southwest of Artheria way out into the great ocean. Their cities are or made of white stone and sit amongst the jungles and hills as if they sat there naturally." Domina could see Kyle was intrigued by her story. "The Abeytu are peaceful for the most part, not a fan of strangers though, hard to make friends"

"How did you become friends?" Kyle asked enthralled by the new land. Domina pulled out a talisman from around her neck. It was a simple necklace made of stones and string. Kyle could see on each stone was a carving of a symbol.

"I was working on a ship a few years back, some scholars wanted to find the people. After about three days sail, we had landed on the northern part of the island. We'd heard stories of the people, but no one had ever found anything." Domina played with the stones in-between her fingers. She moved away from the water taking a swig before sealing it. Domina sat down opposite Kyle and eyed the bread in his hand. Breaking a piece off, Kyle threw it in the hopes she could continue her story.

"While walking along the shore some of us heard screams. So, we went to see what was happening." Domina took another bite from a stale piece of bread.

"Why were they screaming?" Kyle said eagerly.

"Pirates." Domina mumbled as she chewed the food.

"Pirates had started to raid a village on the shore. They were burning huts and were starting to chain up the villagers."

Kyle was dumbstruck. He couldn't imagine the idea of ever chaining someone up to be a slave. He knew that it was happening in the world but never in his home.

"So, what happened?"

"We couldn't let the pirates take the villagers away when we were so close to finding these people. It had taken us days just find this particular village."

"How are the Abeytu so hard to find, they live on the island?" Kyle questioned confused. Domina swallowed the last bite of her supper.

"*They* are not like us at all. They live one with nature, living amongst the wild even the village we came across blended into the coast." She glared, "You wanna know what happened?".

Kyle nodded silently.

"We snuck up to the edge of the village and then attacked." Domina placed the stones back under her top. Kyle could see a little regret in her eye. "We killed most of the pirates and set the villagers free. They took the pirates that we captured and gave us this necklace." Domina breathed a sigh.

"We never found..."

Domina stopped immediately as her senses perked up.

Kyle broke his focus as he looked around, he couldn't hear

anything. Then it clicked, he couldn't hear anything, not the birds in the trees or any wildlife. Sneaking quietly to a boulder behind Kyle, Domina glanced over the ridgeline down into the valley. Just below them in the treeline where the rocky valley started, she made out the dark figures, Shadow Blades. One of them held a bow while the other had a spear, each one scanning the ground for signs of movement. Panic set in as both looked at each other in fear. Domina signalled for Kyle to pack up their food as she peered over the hillside once more.

The Blades crept closer.

With nowhere to go Domina thought of the only move they had left. Kyle watched her as she moved towards the edge of the waterfall. Below the water fell into a cavern under the mountain.

"What do we do now?" Kyle whispered, the panic written across his face. Domina glanced down at the cavern below once again. Kyle could see the plan taking shape in her mind.

"Follow me." She replied quietly. She gripped her sword and bag tightly and in one motion stepped out into the cavern. Kyle's heart leapt into his mouth as she disappeared into the darkness below. Now all alone the panic gripped him tightly as he heard loose rocks roll nearby.

Footstep, Stop.

Footstep, Stop.

The thought of being captured struck him with fear as well as the idea of jumping into an abyss. A battle waged in his head until finally he stepped from behind the rock and stood facing the darkness below. Every fibre of his being was telling him to step away but in the back of his mind, this was the only way. Adrenaline surged through his veins until finally he silenced all thoughts from his head and stepped out. The drop was sudden and fast. He knew it was only seconds but to him, he felt as if he jumped into Hell.

As quickly as he fell, the stop was just as quick. Every part of his body felt as if he had a wall dropped on him as he slammed into the water. All the wind rushed out of his lungs in shock, his arms and leg stung but he was able to use them still. Moving only on instinct and adrenaline Kyle scrambled to the surface. Finally reaching the air, Kyle took the biggest breath in his life. He saw the rim of the cave high above him, his hearing masked by the deafening roar of the waterfall as it hit the rocks beside him. 'Thank Idella' Kyle repeated in his mind as he floated for a moment. His moment of relief was short lived as the water currents slowly pulled him towards another sound that was growing all too familiar. With the fast-fading light Kyle could just make out breaks in the water as the sound of rushing water loudened. Within moments he was dragged down into the rapids. Kyle gasped as he was plunged under the water and ragged by the currents. Every ounce of effort was used to keep him from drowning or breaking upon the rocks. Moments turned to minutes, minutes to hours and he scratched and scrambled against passing rocks to try and drag himself from the torrent. Before he had a chance to grab a hold of anything, Kyle felt an impact on the back of his head, and all turned to black.

"Wake up Kyle, it is not your time." A voice called out from the deep. At first he thought it was Idella watching over him, her gentle voice calming him. A dark void was before him, all the light of the world absent. Kyle tried to raise his hand, but he was unable to move, all he could feel was the searing pain all over his body. The voice called out again as it echoed around him, "Wake up Kyle."

He recognised the voice, it was Domina. With a sudden and violent cough all the water he had swallowed poured out of him, the pain still ever present. Domina was crouched over him, drenched herself. She had tied her hair back crudely.

"Shush, be quiet." Domina whispered trying to cover his mouth. "We're not alone down here." Kyle froze, trying desperately to stop coughing. Every cough caused a pulse to shoot through his head. Just above Domina's head, Kyle could see the light that had crept into the cave, 'We must be near the entrance.'

"Is it the Blades?" Kyle mumbled as he sat up. On his hand he felt the oily consistency of blood. Even at full strength they were no match for the Blades on their own.

"No, they look like marauders or bandits." The relief in her voice didn't do much to calm the fear in his mind. "And it looks like they have horses." Domina said with a grin.

"How many?"

"Not sure but we got to get past them anyway. Might as well take the horses otherwise the Blades will catch up to us." The looming idea of Blades catching them was enough to spur Kyle into doing just about anything.

By the mouth of the cave a dozen bandits were gathered around sorting through the spoils of their last raid.

"Anyone so much as hides any gold for themselves before I've had a chance to count it, I'll feed ya to a Reaper!" One shouted, his voice gravelled. A rough and weathered man, he was dressed in leather bound armour that covered his chest and arms. Underneath, his skin was scarred and covered in warpaint. Even from where they sat, Domina could see he was the leader. He looked at one of the smaller men in his group, "Ya get that lot into the cave, it'll be night soon and I don't wanna be caught out when it's dark."

"What's wrong, scared of a little ghost." Another called out, sparking a snigger and laughter from the men. The leader remained straight faced as he stared down the man.

"I've been raiding before ya were even born!" He growled. His chest puffed up as he took a step forward. His statue rose as if he grew instantly. "There are things out ere you couldn't even dream of, I know what I seen." His eyes shot from one man to the next. The laughter fell silent as he stared them down.

"Beings beyond you and me, I've seen an elemental."

"Bullshit boss." The raider whipped round to see his second, Hal, standing next to a cart. "Elementals are fairy tales, they don't exist."

"I know what I saw, A woman on the wind moving from one place to the next without ever walking."

"A ghost, nothing else." Hal responded amused by the seriousness of their leader. "Maybe it was the God Brima out to get lost souls." The men started to chuckle again. The man grew frustrated as they laughed at him.

"Get back to work, Festus take that into the cave now." The leader pointed before storming off out of the cave.

Domina and Kyle watched as Festus and a couple moved crates and chests further into the cave. Kyle checked the area was clear before Domina moved up. They darted between the crates until they could see the horses in sight. "Almost there." Domina pointed. As she stood up, she came face to face with the bandit leader who looked down on her.

"And who the hell are you two?" He snarled. Domina took a step back at the sight of him. "A couple of thieves we got?"

"Well how are we thieves if you are thieves?" Domina replied. "What makes you think I'm a thief, I'm not the one skulking about?"

"Well, you say we're thieves when actually we haven't stolen anything yet whereas, you have. So, I don't see how you think we're thieves when in fact, can we be thieves of thieves?" The statement stopped the man completely in his tracks. Confused, he struggled to understand what had been proposed.

"Domina." Kyle said worryingly as he looked behind to see the remaining bandits emerge from the mouth of the cave.

"Calm down, I'm making a deal." Domina said as she watched the leader continue to think about the statement. With the bandits closing, each one drawing their weapons, Kyle tugged on her sleeve.

"What?" Domina asked, turning around. Now she saw as she turned back to see their boss had moved from confusion to anger.

"Get em boys!" He shouted. Domina drew her sword and managed to meet the leaders in time. The bandits charged them.

"Kyle do your thing." Domina shouted as she dodged the massive blade of the leader. Kyle drew his sword and managed to deflect one of the oncoming bandits.

"I don't know how to!" He responded in panic. Domina sighed as she darted out of range of her opponent.

"Are you kidding, just fight them."

Domina threw sand into the big man's eyes. Blinded, he stumbled back and was met with a swift kick in his midsection. Kyle frantically blocked and swung his blade catching one across the chest. Falling to the ground, Kyle was stunned by the pain he caused but was knocked to the ground by Hal.

"I like the sword." Hal said as he lifted his weapon above his head, "I'll have it."

Kyle raised his empty hand to protect himself. In a vicious blast of light Hal was thrown far away colliding with the cave wall. His bones cracked under the force of the impact. His lifeless body slumped to the group lifelessly. The other bandits stopped immediately and turned to see Kyle as he stood up. His eyes had a bluish hue and around his hand the Mana wrapped and cracked. Festus, not scared of Kyle, charged once again. In a swift move Kyle swung his arm around and a whip of lightning caught Festus around the neck. Dropping his sword and clawing desperately at his neck the other bandits watched on in terror. Domina and the leader had also stopped in awe of what they were witnessing.

"Run away!" Kyle boomed, his voice hummed with energy. The bandits turned and fled in hysteria, dropping their weapons as they disappeared into the forest. In one motion Kyle pulled on the whip and threw Festus in the direction of the leader. Domina moved just in time to see the two remaining marauders collide. Falling to the floor in a heap, Domina lay stunned on the ground as Kyle walked towards them the power cracking around him.

Taking a deep breath, the Mana slowly dissipated until only the Kyle she had known remained. Looking down at a stunned Domina he offered her his hand.

"Now that!" Domina said in disbelief, "That's how you fight." She looked at his hand for a moment unsure if she would feel the Mana herself.

"I don't know how I did that, I just thought of stopping him and then when the other charged me I thought about grabbing him."

Domina grabbed his hand and jumped to her feet. After seeing what he could do, the plot to take the amulet uncovered another twist in her plan. For now, they were safe and eager to move on.

Leaving the bandit camp behind them, both rode in silence as they collected their thoughts. Kyle tried to process what he'd done, the violence he committed. Domina could see the conflict in him since the fight. Even in the alleyway she knew he'd never fought anyone and after saving her life, Domina knew the least she could do was reassure him.

"Hey, that your first time?" Domina asked.

"I've never killed someone before." Kyle sighed. Domina knew the feeling of a first kill. Only few people in the world ever enjoyed taking a life, something she tried to avoid herself. The only way she knew how to comfort was with harsh truth.

"You read a lot of books? All those heroes on quests?".

Kyle nodded. "How many do you think had to kill someone to complete their quests?" The question stripped away at the varnish of all the stories he had ever read. Arturus and Bellatris, Ajax the great and Bellatris IV all great heroes of battle.

"Look they don't mention this in your books but in the real world, in a real fight, it's kill or be killed." Domina said with sincerity. Despite the harshness of her words, Kyle knew she was right, after all she had managed to survive for so long. All Kyle could do was nod as they continued to ride on. In the distance just above the treeline they could see the town of Clowetta on the banks of the Fellanre lake.

"Look on the Bright side." Domina said with a grin as she looked over at Kyle. "Now we've got the horses the trip's only going to take four days." Domina's grin was infectious as Kyle's sullen mood broke with a grin of his own. Things were starting to look up.

A Den of Thieves
Chapter 20

On the fourth day of their journey across the north, Kyle and Domina had finally reached the outskirts of the province of Shanktown. All across the plains Kyle kept an eye on east, ever conscious of the Blades that pursued him. The land had little in the way of hills or valleys leaving them exposed for miles around but in return allowed them to see anyone else. On the second day of their journey Domina had suggested travelling off the road in a bid to lose their trackers. This had been the longest he'd ever ridden a horse and after the third day he hands started to hurt from the reigns.

Far into the north Kyle could make out the summits of mountains that spanned the whole north like a natural wall. Domina explained to him they were the boundary between the north and the wastes beyond. The wastes had been in folklore across the land as the world's end. His father, Tomen regularly joked about monsters and mythical creatures that roamed there looking for unwary travellers to feed on. His humour was something of an acquired taste to a lot of people in the town, but his mother loved it no the less.

Just below the horizon Domina pointed to a city. "Shanktown, the forgotten city." A gleam in her eye. "If you want adventure and stories this is the place to come." Kyle watched on as the towers in the distance rose further into the sky. As they closed in on the city, he soon saw the city for what it is. Broken and crumbling towers rebuilt with metal and wood, its walls had all but fallen into disrepair.

"I thought Shanktown used to be the city of El Luma?" he said, puzzled. As they finally reached the city the extent of its fallen prestige revealed itself. The buildings mirrored Artheria's in size but not in grandeur, walls were cracked or missing bricks, the roofs of each house had mismatched tiles like a patchwork quilt. Its people fared no better as they were dirtied and most looked of an unsavoury nature. The streets were covered in wet mud and alive with bodies, drunk or dead, Rats scurried about in search of food.

"It was the city of El Luma, but when the Lords abandoned it centuries ago." Domina looked down from her horse as people shuffled about their daily lives. "They left more than just their buildings."

Kyle could feel Domina had an affinity for the people and their struggles. Although not knowing much about her past, in his brief glimpse into the people of Shanktown Kyle dreaded to think what it would have been like to grow up here. Every now and then Kyle spotted a couple of children huddled in doorways, occasionally one attempting to steal from shops or people. Domina smiled as she watched on, reminiscing on her childhood. As they continued further into the city the sound of gulls called out above them.

"Nearing the docks now, I will warn you to keep everything close to you. It's not the friendliest place."

Kyle gripped his sword tighter as grim looks were becoming more common.

"Where is your contact, I don't think we should linger here." Kyle insisted.

The two finally reached a spot on the docks and dismounted. Spread out before them busy docks where the majority of the city's trade had been through and even after centuries it continued to thrive. There was a stark contrast between the buildings around the docks compared to the rest of the dilapidated city. Ships of all shapes and sizes sat against the bustling jetties. The people were as varied as the ships they manned, some common fishermen but Kyle noticed the foreign clothing of some exotic sailors. Flags of all different colours flew on the salty sea breeze that felt fresh against their faces. Domina seemed at peace as she looked upon the sight, Breathing in deep before a long low sigh.

"What do we do now?" Kyle asked as he looked around the streets. The sound of a fisherman calling out to the crowds caught Kyle's attention.

"Freshly caught! Great prices!"

It felt like he was watching his father for a split second. The realisation that he might not see him again started to cloud his mind, so he quickly pushed it to the back of his mind. Now focused back on the present Kyle looked around at everything else.

Sat nearby in a porch of what looked like a tavern was a man that caught his gaze. Sat still and silently, the small but broad man stared intently at Kyle. His clothes were plain but looked toughened for the northern seasons. His face was weathered and set between a heavy brow and shaven beard piercing grey eyes. His stare made Kyle uneasy.

"*We* don't do anything, I'm going to go see if I can find him about the docks." Domina told Kyle. "You need to stay nearby in case we need to leave, there is a tavern over there."

Kyle looked back at the patchwork building whilst trying not to make eye contact with the intimidating man.

"Why don't I stay with you, it'd be much safer?" Kyle hesitated.

"Trust me, stay here, I'll be back soon." Without a chance to debate she was off. In a matter of moments Domina had blended into the crowds of people. Tired and thirsty Kyle took her suggestion and wandered over to the tavern hearing the rising sound of chanting and cheering coming from inside.

Inside the smell of blood, sweat and other unsightly things hung closely in the air. With every breath Kyle felt sick as he made his way through the crowds. In the centre of the floor a large wooden balcony overlooked a fight pit below. Kyle caught a glimpse of the action as two fighters fought to the cheers of the crowd. With each punch or kick the crowd cheered and booed, men called out odds on each as they exchanged money with the crowds. With a thunderous cheer as the larger of the two fighters felled his opponent with a furious strike to the face. He roared victoriously at the masses as his opponent was dragged out of the pit. After a moment another man entered the arena, dressed in a long fancy coat that made him stand out from everyone in the room. The coat much like the rest of the city may have been once for the lords of the city, now just patchworked and beat.

"Another crushing victory for the champion of Shanktown!" The announcer shouted to the crowd. His voice echoed and boomed over the crowd as they reacted to the statement. "Who has any hope of defeating this monstrous mountain of a man?" The announcer looked back to the giant who nodded, a trickle of blood coming from a scratch on his forehead.

"Ladies and gentlemen, the Titan himself is ready for another challenge, who among dares to defeat the titan and claim the prize?"

The crowd chattered and muttered amongst themselves as they looked around each other until a voice popped up. "I will."

The accent struck Kyle with curiosity. It was unlike any he'd ever heard as the man walked out from the crowd into the pit. The tanned man was significantly smaller than the Titan, slimmer and toned. He walked with confidence as he stood in the centre eyeing up the champion. "So, we have another opponent for the Titan." The announcer spoke as he walked towards the entrance. He sneered at the challenger. "Let's see if he becomes another victim to the Titan." With a slam behind him the gates shut. The challenger removed his shirt and dropped it to the ground. His body was covered in tattoos and scars, his every muscle defined as he moved. Standing in the centre defiantly the Titan stared and chuckled to himself at the sight of his opponent. Waving for the challenger to step forward the Titan took a step forward. With a huge swing the Titan missed as the challenger stepped out of the way. More and more he swung and more and more the challenger danced around him each time landing a kick or punch. His catlike agility made the Titan mad as he tried to corner his opponent. In a swift kick the tattooed challenger struck the Titan in the groin dropping him to his knees. The Crowd hissed in imagined pain as they looked on at their injured champion. The challenger saw the opportunity and forced his knee into the face of the Titan. Blood blew from his nose as he fell back crashing to the floor. The crowd fell silent in bewilderment. The challenger calmly looked around the crowd who started to cheer at the carnage.

For half an hour Kyle sat at a table, drinking and eating what little food he could order. The crowds were ever louder as the fighting continued.

"You look lost." A voice grumbled. Kyle looked up to see the small stocky man staring at him. Now so close he could see the weathering on his face, his eyes as dark as the night. "You shouldn't be here."

"I'm just passing through." Kyle stuttered. "I'm not looking for trouble."

The man scoffed at the remark. "It's the ones that don't look for trouble that find it."

Kyle noticed the scarred skin on the man's jaw, the lines built up one on top of the other. The intimidating stare made Kyle shudder. He knew that he needed to find Domina.

"I think I'll leave now." He stammered. As Kyle stood up the man caught a glimpse of the amulet in his rucksack. He looked surprised at Kyle who now feared what the man would do.

"You may want to be careful young one, many have gotten lost in this city." The man grunted. He looked from under his heavy brow at Kyle.

"Duŕum Kél" he spoke. The words were sharp and harsh enough for Kyle to understand their tone. Without another thought Kyle swiftly moved to the door and left.

Kyle instantly felt calmer as the sea air washed over his face. He breathed deeply and slowly exhaled, the anxiety leaving each time. His meditation abruptly interrupted as he felt a hand land on his back causing him to spin rapidly, Mana started to course through his eyes.

"Calm down, it's me." Domina whispered hoping no one saw the display of power. "Stop that or someone will see."

Kyle calmed down again as he looked around at the people passing, each one oblivious to his sudden outburst.

"Where were you?" Kyle snapped as she looked around suspiciously.

"I said I was looking for my contact and I found him." She said defensively. "They're waiting for us."

"They?" Kyle stressed. "Who are 'they'?"

"Some monks from the looks, they're here to take the amulet to a safe place."

Kyle felt unsure about the identity of the people. Too many people were becoming involved in his quest, he started to wonder who to trust. Domina saw the doubt beginning to linger in his eyes as he thought to himself.

"Look we've come this far, these people can help us keep that safe."

Kyle was pleased to see Domina interested in keeping the amulet safe, even if she was being paid to do it. 'Honour among sell swords' Kyle thought to himself but still felt sceptical. Still seeing Kyle needed a bit more convincing she thought back to Artheria and the scholar he met with.

"They received word from Felix."

The mention of Felix dispelled a lot of the doubt in his mind. 'Maybe Felix knew about the broken bridge and sent his friend to come to Shanktown.'

"Where do we go?"

Domina smiled and extended her hand out towards a street off the docks. The two walked along the waterway together all the while under the watchful eyes of the short man.

Knife in the Dark
Chapter 21

The road had been long and arduous but finally he had made it to his destination. Kyle thought back to his encounters with the Shadow Blades and the near misses. The most memorable for him was the sights he'd seen as he finally recalled seeing Artheria in the morning sun or the Aurora flowing through the night sky, each one a marvel he would remember forever. Finally, he had reached the end of his quest and would soon be heading home to his family and Lucia. With that in mind, Kyle still couldn't help but be reminded of the words Idella, or whoever she was, about the visions. Each night they would play out in his mind, but they still didn't make sense to him.

Domina and Kyle had left the docks and now walked towards a large building set away from everything. Dock workers and merchants constantly tried to stop them to sell their wares as they walked through the crowded streets. Domina dismissed them with ease until they reached the stone building. It stood out from its neighbouring buildings, it's walls had remained intact, and the roof was complete, a rare sight in the city. With two large fists against the door Domina stepped back. Kyle heard the bolts and chains unlock from the inside as a large man opened the door. Kyle was in awe of the man as he stood nearly seven-foot-tall with broad shoulders and a large belly to match. His heavy eyes were matched with a dull expression on his face. Domina looked at him seemingly unphased.
"We're here to see your master." Domina said.

He looked them both up and down before slowly standing aside to let them in. As Kyle passed through the door, he could see the extent of how large the man was, stooping to avoid hitting his head on the roof. Further in the room, Domina came to rest on a counter where an older man stood with a smile on his face. The room was covered in manner of items, walls adorned with rugs, paintings, weapons all exotic, all wonderous.

"Welcome Kyle, you must be tired from your travels. Let me introduce myself, I'm Masamo Terventus." He spoke as he shook Kyle's hand. He wore a fine blue tunic and had fine dark boots. On one of his fingers was a ring, a serpent with two emerald eyes. "You've obviously met my associate Hep" signally to the giant at the door.

"Hep" the giant repeated with a grin on his face pointing to himself.

"What does that mean?" Kyle wondered.

"It's his name." Domina replied. "He doesn't say anything else, doesn't know how to say anything else." She chuckled as Hep gave her a big hug before sitting down in an oversized chair. Every footstep he made the floor shuck a little.

"Is he...?"

"Giant?" Masamo interjected. "No, although I wouldn't be surprised if he had it in his blood."

"Do giants even exist?" Kyle asked as he looked over at Hep. Hep smiled to himself as a cat jumped up onto his lap and brushed up against the gentle giants' hands.

"They used to, but no one has seen any in centuries." Masamo answered.

"You hear stories in taverns or on the docks, but the people are usually drunk or they mistake something for something else." Domina added.

"Speaking of stories, Domina has been telling me about your story."

Masamo stood up from behind the counter. A look of intrigue settled on his face. "Please let me see the item."

Kyle looked at Domina with hesitation, the anxious feelings started to play on his mind again. Domina nodded but still Kyle's instincts tugged at him.

"Domina said that you know Felix's contact?" Kyle deflected the request. His instinct wrenched in his gut as he held firmly onto his rucksack. "How do I know *they* are they right people?"

Domina felt the tension between Masamo and Kyle rise. She knew Kyle was nervous about revealing the amulet, but she had managed to get so far.

"They said they were from the Cyrillian order." Masamo said calmly as he placed a piece of cloth down on the table. Inked onto the cloth Kyle recognised the symbol from Felix's study. "They have travelled from Beltoria to retrieve the item."

The mention of the Cyrillian order with the emblem helped sway the hesitation in his mind as he moved to the counter. Watching Masamo intently, he pulled the amulet from his bag and held it in his hand. The expression on Masamo's face had become one Kyle had come to expect when viewing the amulet. Masamo inspected it from a distance as he moved from side to side, the shine of the light bounced off the polished gold.

"Right this way." Masamo ushered to a doorway to his right.

Recoiling the amulet, Kyle placed it into his bag and looked at Domina. Rolling her eyes, Domina stood up from the counter and made her way into the doorway and down the stairs. Kyle glanced back at Masamo who continued to smile and bow his head.

The stairs down to the lower floor were narrow and low. Recesses were carved into the walls to allow candles to light the stairway. The shadows cast by the brick walls made Kyle feel caged as he delved deeper into the darkness. After a moment the stairs opened into a large hall with a wooden balcony, similar to the tavern Kyle had been in. On the roof a large iron grate allowed light to stream in through the bars, illuminating the centre leaving the edges of the room dark. In the centre of the room two figures stood in hooded white cloaks. Kyle struggled to see their faces because of the light which forced him to come to a stop in front of them before he could make out their faces.

"May I introduce Kemina and Dora of the Cyrillian Order." Masamo announced as the monks bowed their heads to Kyle. "And may I present to you, Kyle of Rheia." Kyle, unsure about the etiquette of the situation bowed his head in response. Domina however stood at the side between the light and shadow. Kyle glanced over; he noticed a troubled look on her face momentarily before snapping out of her vacant stare.

"Greetings Kyle, we must commend you on your resolve to protect the amulet, a feat that I fear would not have been possible in anyone else's hands. Brother Felix indeed choose wisely." Kemina acknowledged.

"Thank you, my lord, I wished to fulfil my teacher's final request." Kyle graciously accepted Kemina's judgement.

"Do you have the amulet?" Dora asked his voice low and gravelled which sounded familiar to Kyle. The feeling in his stomach had not dissipated since he arrived, now however it started to stir. Reluctantly Kyle lowered his bag and opened it. Holding the amulet into the light, its jewels casting the light around the room. Kemina took a few paces forward to look at the amulet in more detail. Her feminine features were revealed by the light as she removed her hood.

"It is indeed the amulet of Bellatris. The order will be most pleased."

Kemina took hold of the amulet and continued to inspect it as she walked back to Dora's side.

"It was most unfortunate that Master Pret was killed during the attack but now his charge has been completed, torture is a terrible way to go."

Kyle suddenly stopped at the mention of Pret. In all the retelling of how he came to have the amulet, he had never mentioned how Pret had died to anyone.

"Now that the item has been safely delivered, I think I'm owed some pay." Domina demanded as she took a step forward into the light.

"How do you know Master Pret was tortured may I ask?" Kyle interrupted.

"Of course, we were made aware of it by way of Brother Felix."

Kyle's suspicions started to fill in the blanks of his doubts. For a while he felt uneasy about the idea of coming to Shanktown and the misinformation had confirmed the bad choice.

"Forgive me, my lord, I never mentioned how Master Pret died to anyone, not even Felix." Kyle clarified.

"You must be mistaken young one." Dora hesitantly replied. Kyle could hear a quiver in his voice.

"No, I remember clearly. The only way you could have known is…"

"…I had killed him myself." A voice boomed out from the darkness. Emerging from the shadows, Keela walked into the light. The scars on his face were deep from the harsh shadows. Kyle felt dread at the sight of him. Kyle looked to

Domina who fear had replaced her confidence as she looked at Keela.

"I delivered the amulet as promised. Now I'm owed payment." Domina demanded. The betrayal Kyle felt could not be put into words as he stared at her, his jaw open.

"Your payment is your life." Ariel responded as she appeared behind Domina, a knife wrapped around her throat. "Be thankful you get to keep it." Ariel pulled the knife away and pushed Domina away.

Kyle continued to track Domina as she walked past him without a look, too ashamed of her actions. Masamo bowed to Keela and followed Domina closely behind. His heart sank to point he'd never felt before. Keela saw the defeat in Kyle's eyes as he stared at the ground.

"You are probably wondering why she betrayed you? To build your trust, travel so far with you only to deliver you to us?" Keela smiled as he held the amulet in his hand. "Greed. Greed is a disease in this world, everyone has darkness in them and one way or another it finally comes to light."

Keela began to circle Kyle.

"Your Master Pret, Felix, all taught you that in this world the hero always wins, saves the day and defeats evil. All the while omitting the truth of things." Keela came to a stop facing Kyle. He could see a Kyle welling up, tears filling his eyes.

"You failed because you are not a hero, this is not a fairy tale, and we are not bandits."

Kemina and Dora disrobed to show the dark clothes they wore underneath. Above them on the balcony a few more Blades appeared from the shadows. Keela passed the amulet to Ariel who placed it into her top.

"You failed because you cannot face the power of Nightshade and hope to win." Keela continued to dominate Kyle. "Just like your father could never have defeated me."

Whatever Keela's game of goading was, it was enough for Kyle, instantly he felt the rage build up in his body. His eyes glowed blue, burning away the tears as his hands cracked with lightnning. Overcome with anger Kyle lashed out at Keela with a whip of blue lightning but was cut down with ease. The power drained from him as his anger turned to sorrow and defeat.

"Just like your father." Keela scoffed, "You are a boy trying to play with gods."

Keela turned to Kemina and Dora, their weapons at the ready. "Deal with him then kill the girl and the old man." Keela commanded for Ariel to follow him as they disappeared into the darkness. Dora stood above Kyle with bad intent. His face was burnt, and part of his hair had been scorched.

"I may not have killed your mother, but I'll make you pay for what she did to me."

Kyle felt the rage overwhelm him again as he reached for his sword and struck out. Catching Dora in his arm, Kemina retaliated by slashing at Kyle. Kyle thought about the Bandits and how he managed to beat them. His instincts kicked in and he motioned to grab Kemina. Lightning lashed out from his hand wrapped around her neck. Before he could do anything, Dora threw himself at Kyle knocking him to the ground. The two struggled against each other as they rolled on the ground trying to gain the advantage.

The blades above jumped down to assist their brethren but were met with the sound of breaking iron. Above them a shadow landed in the middle of the room and with a swing of an axe he caught one of the Blades in the chest.

The force was enough to throw the Shadow Blade back against the wall, a cavity in his chest. Kyle saw it was the short man. He swung his Axe with ferocity as he attacked the Blades. Kyle now with help focused his thoughts on Dora who now had managed to gain the upper hand. Knocking Kyle's hands out of the way Dora now wrapped his hands around Kyle's neck and squeezed.

The air stopped as Kyle gasped frantically. Images of his family flashed in his mind, Tomen lying dead on the floor, Lucia smiling at him. All these memories caused him to refocus enough to strike one last time. The Mana coursed through his hands as Kyle reached for Dora's head. He screamed in agony as the power surged through his head, stumbling to his feet. Kyle managed to make it to his knees but could feel the power overtaking his control, the Mana turning his blue veins white. The short man saw the glow emitting from Kyle who started to struggle with the pain. Pulse.

Pulse.

Pulse. The surges grew quicker and more intense with each passing second.

After knocking another Blade to the ground, the short man ran for the stairs. The glow increased consuming Kyle, now no longer could hold on. Screaming as a blinding powerful wave burst from his body, it ripped through stone, wood and metal as it destroyed the building around him. The citizens of Shanktown ran in panic as the building detonated under their feet, throwing everything out. Chunks of stone and wood rained down in the streets as foundations continued to crumble into the hole created. The violent tremors slowly subsided as the once proud building now laid in ruins, the neighbouring buildings crumbled from the force of the earthquake.

Domina laid on the ground confused by the sudden eruption that had knocked her off her feet. People ran past her screaming and crying at the destruction that had unfolded. She turned back to see smoke rising from where she had been. In front of her the docks were awash as the tide engulfed the lower sections of the wooden jetties. She clambered to a nearby doorway to escape the stampeding crowds. She had managed to escape with her life not only from Ariel but the explosion that now had devastated the city. For the first time she felt conflicted.

"Fire, the fire is spreading!" One citizen shouted.

For Domina she had always looked out for herself 'no one bothered with me' she reminded herself every day. Survival was the priority, getting rich was the bonus. This time it was different, she had never had to lead someone to their death. Over the years, the lines of morality disappeared one by one, each time she justified them 'survival of the smartest'. This time however, her conscience though distant in her mind, now screamed out to her. It kicked and screamed like a prisoner desperate to escape.

"Get up Domina." She muttered to herself. "Get out of here."

She pulled herself to her feet and dusted off the dust that hung in the air. Stepping out among the crowds of people, she saw a short man calmly walking away from the disaster carrying someone on his back.

It was Kyle.

Dumbstruck as to how Kyle had survived the building's collapse, she watched on as the short man rushed away towards the outskirts of the docks.

Domina pushed and fought against the crowds to follow the man as he now hurried through the streets. At times she struggled to see them as they blended in with the chao in the streets. Catching a glimpse of Kyle's limp body, she quickened her pace to close the distance but fought hard against the crowds that pushed back. She reached the end of the street that opened up into the docks and the river beyond, Domina scanned the streets either side. Rowing in haste, the short man stared at Domina their eyes locked. Domina knew that she had few moral lines left to cross, Kyle had been the first that she regretted. Now was the time to change that.

Guardian Angel
Chapter 22

The smell of smoke-filled Kyle's nose as it blew across his face. The wind gently flowing through the knee-high grass that he laid in. As he opened his eyes a familiar sight welcomed him. He realised he was back on the clifftop, where Idella had first come to him. The sky however looked different as he slowly sat up. High above a distant mountain, a portal circled around its peak. The event horizon morphed with purples, blues and red and at its centre a black void. Standing overlooking the vista Idella watched the rising smoke. As if she knew, Idella turned around to look at Kyle, a great sadness on her face.

"What's happening?"

"Things are now in motion that cannot be stopped." She responded softly. Kyle looked away in shame.

"I've failed you, I failed everyone."

Idella stepped away from the cliff edge and gracefully moved towards Kyle. Kneeling down, she gently lifted Kyle's face up to hers.

"No, you have not, this is just a glimpse of what could happen. You have a strength in you that you have only begun to explore."

Kyle tried to look away as Idella lowered her hand.

"What good is Mana if the person I thought I could trust brought me to Nightshade's followers? How can I fight against two sides?"

"Who said anything about Mana?" Idella chuckled, her laugh brought a physical glow to her face.

"You have strength in you that very few people have, true courage. It is in this strength people are drawn to you and in the coming struggles, will stand by you."

Kyle finally turned his gaze to Idella and looked her in the eyes. Now he was close enough, Kyle finally saw her eyes were different, the iris changed hues from soft greens, purples and blues.

"What about Domina? I thought I could trust her; how can I stand against Nightshade if the people at my side do what she did?" Kyle asked. Even in her presence he could feel his courage waver. "I can't do this alone."

Idella stood up, her dress wafting in the breeze.

"You will not be alone. Your path has only just begun, and you will share it with many peoples of this world. Trust in yourself, believe in yourself and those people will come to believe in you as I do."

A stronger gust of wind blew past, and she burst into petals and blossoms that floated away.

***

The slow dip of water echoed around Kyle as his senses slowly returned to him. Each drip was replied with a splash in a nearby puddle. The smell of must filled his lungs as he opened his eyes. Every inch of his body ached causing him to groan as he sat up, his head pounding in time with his heartbeat. The dark limestone caves were coated in water that seeped down into the ground which had become a playground of mosses and fungi everywhere. Light filtered in from an opening up ahead that allowed Kyle to scan his surroundings. 'Where am I now?' he thought exhaustedly. Memories of the confrontation with the Blades flooded back to him. Between the visions and waking up, Kyle imagined he might finally have arrived in the underworld. Kyle looked at his arms to see if the Mana was still glowing. Just before the explosion of energy it had felt as if he had been thrown into a fire, the ends of his nerves burning. With no sight of Mana on his body or stirring feelings, only the pain of his power, Kyle tried to get to his feet. A quiet murmur could just be heard over the trickling water.

"Duŕum Kél vas am Tet, Duŕum Kél Khazad sul
Zhar Fhund Mak-el, nhar tyrne xine"
(Protector of the spirit, Protector of city
Guide me in my journey, for the world is dark)

The guttural words repeated as Kyle cautiously made his way further into the cave. A lantern hung brightly on a rusted hook that was driven into the cave wall. The light allowed Kyle to see the short man on his knees in what seemed to be prayer to a Rune carved into the wall. The man was topless allowing his tattoos to be seen across the whole of his body. Kyle marvelled at the detail of them as each one connected to the next one, a mixture of runes and figures. Kyle recognized the man from the tavern which only now added to the confusion in his mind. "How did I get here?" Kyle groaned. The man calmly finished his ritual without so much of a flinch before turning to look at Kyle. His heavy brow cast a heavier shadow over his eyes.

"I pulled you from the rubble Duŕum." He grunted. "Your display was powerful but stupid."

Kyle felt embarrassed by the backhanded compliment. Even as he tried to understand his gift, it also found a way to control him.

"Who are you?" Kyle asked nervously. "I recognised you from the tavern but as I said I have nothing to give."

The man moved to his things that were neatly piled on a nearby the rock. Kyle continued to focus on the man's tattoos until he placed his garments back on, and something clicked in Kyle's mind. Kyle remembered the book he borrowed from Master Pret and the last city of the Dwarves.

"You're a Dwarf?" Kyle exclaimed. His nervousness turned to excitement. The man growled as continued to dress. "I thought your kind were whipped out during the Dawning war. The Dwarf sharply turned.

"Choose your words wisely Ghárd," He growled. Kyle was frozen in place by the black eyes that locked on him. "Dwarves are the masters of stone and metal; it'd be wise not to anger one."

Kyle now felt the books that spoke of Dwarven ferocity did not do them justice. His over excitement at meeting one of the marvellous people was too much for his nerves to battle as questions poured into his mind.

"Forgive me, but I thought Dwarves had beards?" The Dwarf rolled his eyes as he picked up his axe and marched past Kyle to the mouth of the cave.

"The ignorance of man never ceases to amaze me." The Dwarf muttered. Kyle felt ashamed he had bombarded the man with questions, both seemed to have insulted the man, and not thought to ask the name of his saviour.

"I'm sorry I never thanked you for saving me from the Blades." Kyle groaned again as a sharp pain shot up his side. The Dwarf nodded as he glanced back at Kyle. "What is your name?"

"Ezekiel." He replied as went back to looking out the cave. Kyle came to a stop by the entrance. The land before them was hilly and covered in sharp black rocks that looked like obsidian. The rain had poured for some time creating streams and waterfalls that ran off into the valley. The weather looked as bleak as Kyle felt knowing Keela had finally taken the amulet from him. All the travelling and running had been for nothing as Kyle thought about the vision Idella had shown him. 'The world will burn and it's all my fault' he told himself. Ezekiel looked over to Kyle whose emotions spoke louder than any words.

"Forget about what's happened, we need to be moving now." He spoke.

"How can I forget; the amulet was taken and now he will release Nightshade." Kyle stressed. "The world is going to end and I'm the reason why. Keela was right. I'm no hero." Kyle felt a tear start to fill his eye. He dreamed of being like the heroes of old. Ezekiel stood up firmly. The weight of his clothes and body looked intimidating without words.

"Look out at the world, is it dead?" He asked. Kyle looked and shook his head. "Then the world is not dead, and we can still do something."

"What are we going to do?"

"We go north into the mountains."

'Why go north?' He wondered, nothing is there but folklore creatures and snow.

"What's in the north, it's just snow."

Ezekiel ignored the question and moved towards Kyle's sword. With all the stone and rubble that crushed him, Kyle was confused as to how even he managed to survive. He looked that his father's sword and smiled. 'At least that managed to survive.

"How did I survive the building? Surely it would have killed me."

"Do all your people ask these many questions, or is it just you?" Ezekiel snapped. Kyle could see he had a short temper to match his demeanour.

"Just me I suppose." Kyle stuttered. Ezekiel sighed and leant on his axe.

"When I pulled the rubble off, the stone had formed a dome over you as if something held it in place. I pulled you up and carried you here. Does that answer your question?"

Kyle nodded his head. He refrained from asking any of the other questions that kept springing in his mind. Ezekiel's patience was starting to wear thin as he kept looking out towards the open world. Satisfied for now Kyle achingly stood up and strapped his sword to his waist. They both left the safety of the cave into the downpour.

The journey was uncomfortable not only for the razor-sharp rocks that stuck out in the path, but the silence Ezekiel had insisted on since leaving the cave. The wilderness of the hills felt different to Kyle compared to the mountains he had visited already. The untouched landscape felt ancient and primordial, green moss like grass grew on the black stones. A waterfall fell in the distance on a wide open plain, its spray carrying on the wind. With nothing much to say Kyle wandered the wasteland behind Ezekiel. In all his wildest dreams he never thought he would see a Dwarf let alone meet one and now he was in the company of one, he studied every detail of him as they climbed the peak. For most of the climbing Ezekiel used his axe as a cane helping pull his heavy frame up the hill, his clothes were ordinary just like anyone else that might call the north their home. Apart from his short but broad frame the only thing that hinted at his true origins was the tattoos on his body. Kyle tried to recall the details of them, each rune surrounded by angular patterns.

Ezekiel threw his hand up immediately as he heard the faint sound of rolling rocks. Kyle thought the worst and grabbed his sword, their eyes up above them. Both scanned the ridges of the rocks to see where exactly the ominous sound originated. Ezekiel quietly sniffed the air as a faint scent caught his nose.

"Let's keep moving." He commanded. Kyle was still cautious as he lingered for a moment before setting off. After walking all day, the intimidating hill finally started to give way to small valleys leading into the barren white wastes. The rain that had soaked them for hours turned cold and eventually into snow. The stories about the wastes so far had been exactly true about the north, cold, barren and lifeless. Kyle thought they must have been the only living things for miles around.

"How far are we going?" Kyle shuddered, the cold had permeated his clothes to his very core. "I don't think I can go much more; it's freezing."

Ezekiel ignored Kyle's questions coming to a stop on a large rock. He looked out over the wastes before them and waved Kyle to join him.

"That's where we are going, not far left." Ezekiel replied, pointing to a ruin half buried in snow. At the base of the valley the ruin had long seen the harshness of the wastes and weather but somehow the majority of its stonework was still standing. Ezekiel turned and jumped off the rock landing with a thud, the ice under the shallow snow cracked under his boots. Kyle started to become frustrated.

"You still haven't told me why we're going here." Since the start of his journey Kyle had been sent or led to places he knew little about, each time it ended badly for him. Since losing the amulet his frustration started to build into anger. "I have to say thank you for saving me, but I'm not going any further until you tell me why we are going there." Ezekiel turned to glare over his shoulder. Despite the intimidating look Kyle was determined. "If you want to help me stop Keela, they will be halfway to Telloma not up here."

The emotional outburst produced little response from the Dwarf who continued to stare at him. After a moment of complete silence Ezekiel thrust his axe into the ground and bound back up the hill towards Kyle. The sight of a Dwarf marching towards him caused him to take a step back.

"We are being followed." Ezekiel whispered, "They have been following us for hours."

Kyle looked around at the snow-capped hills. In all directions the snow was undisturbed. Kyle couldn't see any sign of anyone or anything apart from them.

"I don't see anyone." Kyle replied unconvinced. Ezekiel turned and grabbed his axe and began his descent down the hill.

"I think that's the point!" He shouted. "We are heading this way because it will take us to where we need help."

The ambiguous statement didn't do much to sway Kyle's frustration. Ezekiel turned and bounded back down the hill yanking his axe out of the ground with ease. Kyle looked around one more time before setting off down the hill himself.

The Footsteps of Doom
Chapter 23

It had been eighty years of searching. Pain, blood and death littered his past but finally he held the object of his future in his hand. The amulet of Bellatris was as enticing as he imagined. Forty years ago, he had come close to capturing this treasure but unfortunately a wayward explorer had managed to best him. Keela studied every detail on its golden surface with such focus he had been silent for days. On the edge of the forest Keela, Ariel and the remaining blades camped before pushing into the forest and their final destination, Telloma. The Blades were sat around the camp talking amongst themselves as Keela sat away from them all.

"Kemina and Dora have not returned." Ariel spoke as she entered the camp. She looked to Keela for any sign of concern for their missing brethren but to no avail. Keela remained entranced by the amulet.

"Then we wait, they will come." One replied.

"We push on at dawn." Keela raised his voice. The group looked to Keela who now glanced at them with a spark in his eye. "We are so close to our goal, our destiny." The excitement in his voice was palpable. "We cannot delay fate."

The group looked on stunned by his apathy for his missing followers as he turned back to the amulet. Ariel could feel the confusion of the group and ordered them to rest.

"My Love we must wait for the others to return, are you not concerned they haven't returned?" Ariel said quietly as she sat beside him. For decades Keela had been focused on obtaining the items needed to release Nightshade by any means, but he always showed some compassion for his brothers and sisters. Now that he had the item it was as if he no longer saw Ariel or the others.

"You need to rest." She spoke softly raising, her hand to his. Keela saw the lovingness in her eyes.

"I can't sleep not when we are so close." Keela replied. "I have spent every moment of my life looking for this and now I have the chance to become more powerful than ever, to change the world and create a paradise for us." Keela released his hold on the amulet and grasped Ariel's hand.

"Soon we will have a chance to make the world as we see fit, to be the rulers of all that will last for thousands of years."

Keela's ambition was the first thing Ariel fell in love with the moment she met him almost a century before. In his youth Keela was charismatic and fearless in his adventures and even now he had lost none of it.

"Do you not fear Nightshade will destroy the world? I fear the being inside you is taking its toll on you." Concern grew in Ariel.

"When we release him, he will be weakened and that is when I will take his power." He whispered confidently glancing down at the dagger on Ariel's side, "Trust me, soon I will drain Nightshade of all power and we can be together."

Keela moved towards Ariel and tenderly kissed her. The two embraced for a moment, all the world and darkness faded until only one another were in each other's mind.

Surprises Come in Threes
Chapter 24

Ezekiel and Kyle finally reached the snow-covered ruin at the bottom of the valley. The snow fell heavier and thicker as the evening drew in. On the barren snowscape Kyle saw the outlines of a creature plodding west, judging by its size and how far away it was the creature must be huge he thought. That was not the only thing on his mind though as he followed Ezekiel into the entrance of the ruin. The temperature had fallen again, and Kyle struggled to keep any part of him warm. He worried that if they didn't find shelter soon, he might meet his end at the edge of the world. Huge bronze doors were frozen open and covered in ice. Inside the building remained strong in the harsh winter, it's stone surfaces smooth as marble and as light as sandstone. The layout looked oddly familiar, similar to the stronghold Baradis but didn't have a tower at its centre. Instead, a stone circle stood in the centre upon a raised pedestal. Curious about the circle Kyle moved closer to see markings on its surface. They looked similar to so of the writing he'd seen at Felix's house but different in places. As he reached out to touch the stone Kyle could feel a familiar hum.

"Is this a Dwarven ruin?" Kyle asked looking back at Ezekiel.

"No but we helped build this thousands of years ago when Cyrillian's travelled the world."

"Travelled? How?" Kyle questioned.

"Wait here, I'll be back."

Without a chance to ask, Ezekiel had wandered further into the ruin. Kyle now alone again felt another chill on the wintery breeze, his face and hands already red and tender.

The clothes he'd taken from Felix had served well but struggled to withstand the chill of being so far north. Desperate to find a place to warm up Kyle explored the ruin himself. Epitaphs and depictions were chiselled onto the wall like the ones at the monastery on Ault. The carvings showed a great city surrounded by eight towers and at its centre a light. The detail astounded Kyle as he ran his fingers along the carving.

***

Ezekiel trudged along a path to a building across the courtyard. The snow now deepened as it came up to his elbows. He muttered in Dwarvish to himself, cursing at the snow that slowed him down. Living among Humans for years, he still hated the imprecision of their words, never conveying the meaning he felt. Still the company of Humans entertained him when he visited Shanktown, trivial disputes, drunken fights all amused him in his eyes. He missed the company of his kin on some nights, thinking of his home and the warm fires. It would be years before he thought he would ever be able to go back. 'Dwarves remember' a sentiment his father reminded him of everyday. As he reached the door and the snow receded to his ankles, he spotted the tracks of a giant creature. Kneeling, Ezekiel investigated the prints, pressing into the sides and centre. 'The tracks are still warm' he thought. The track was at least a metre between each paw and each as wide as a shovel.

A Sabre Bear. That was not his only concern, the whiff of a familiar smell caught his nose again. The Bear may have left the safety of the ruin, but they were not alone. A passing of a shadow above him caught his eye as he refrained from turning, maintaining his composure.

Glancing over his shoulder, Ezekiel continued to press onto the door and entered.

Inside the small building was a dimly lit crypt. The circular room had high marble walls with a pedestal at its centre. A shaft of light beamed down from an opening in the ceiling illuminating a silver object laying on top of the pedestal. Hastily Ezekiel picked up the object and placed it into his pocket.

Kyle managed to fit into a small, covered area that protected him from the harsh winds. He crouched with his back against the wall looking out at the stone circle in the courtyard. 'When they travelled?' Kyle pondered. The Cyrillian's controlled Laxos centuries ago but why would they travel here? He felt so cold, trying to answer his own questions tired him easily. For now, the only thing that he really tried to think of was keeping warm. He imagined being back in his house, sat by the fire whilst his family set the table for supper. A smiled curled in the corner of his lips but in the corner of his eye, Kyle caught a glimpse of a shadow in the falling snow. His focus pushed the memory aside as he watched it dart from column to column a tall and slender figure. His mind went into overdrive as he suddenly felt all his energy increase. His mind instantly thought the Blades had found him, 'how did they find me?' Kyle readied his sword, he cold bite at the tips of his fingers. Even if he knew he wasn't a hero as he wanted, He would fight, nonetheless. The shadow crept closer through the snow. Kyle gripped his sword as tight as he could be ready to swing.

Adrenaline kicked as he felt his heart race, his senses in excess.

The shadow was now only a couple metres away as it moved behind the column nearest him.

Now was his moment to strike, slash before they had a chance to strike at him. With a hard swing of his sword the shadow ducked in time and spun around. Standing in front of him as if he'd seen a ghost, was Domina. Kyle was shocked to see her standing before him. Domina could see the look of shock and speechlessness on his face but not enough to stop him holding his sword to her throat. Feeling the sharp blade close to her neck, Domina raised her hands in peace.

"How about we put the sword down." Domina pleaded. Kyle felt his anger for her trying to push him forward whilst his conscience held him back.

"Give me one reason why I don't strike you down." Kyle growled. For the first time he displayed a new side of himself, one which Domina didn't expect from someone like him.

"Because that's not who you are." She replied apologetically.

"You betrayed me!" He screamed.

She had met many men in her life, some were killers through and through. They knew nothing other than that and others were drunks, perverted or greedy. For the first time in her life, she had met someone truly honourable and kind, only to forget those qualities because of what she did.

"I did what I needed to do to survive, I didn't know they were going to kill you." She confessed, "I didn't even know they were there until Masamo introduced them."

Kyle listened to her confession but struggled to believe her.

"You look like you've survived all this time or your own, surely you could have run away?" Kyle fired but he held his anger back.

All the time they were together now made it difficult for him to believe her. She could see Kyle still didn't or wouldn't believe her even if she told him the truth, but she had to.

"Some people even I can't hide from," Domina said softly, "the white woman she…"

A quiet whistle caught their attention as a dart pierced her neck. Confused, she looked into the courtyard to see Ezekiel holding a pipe in one hand. The sedative quickly took effect as Domina began to stumble and waver. All her senses shut down one by one until she finally collapsed to the floor. Appearing from the snow, Ezekiel came to stop above Domina who continued to fight against the effects of the drugs.

"What did you do?" Kyle asked, still trying to process the last few minutes.

"She's been following us since Shanktown. We need to tie her up."

"Where did you go?"

Ezekiel pulled the silver rod from his coat pocket. It was covered in a series of groves that had been poked out.

"Needed this, help me tie her up Durum, we can't have her follow use when we leave."

"You want to leave her here tied up? She'll die." Kyle felt anger for her, but he didn't want to kill her, especially when she had no way of defending herself.

"How is that going to help us travel?" He asked pointing to the rod. Ezekiel finished tying up Domina and pushed her up against the wall. As was his usual response Ezekiel ignored Kyle's question and walked towards the stone circle.

Kyle's frustration grew as he stormed after Ezekiel.

Kneeling at the base of the circle Ezekiel scratched away at the ice that had formed to uncover a slot that fit the shape of the rod. Placing it in he quickly stepped to the side and began to touch individual runes carved onto the circle. Kyle stopped immediately as he saw the runes that had been touched begin to glow purple as the aurora above them. The circle hummed into life as the cracks and runes glowed before a portal burst into existence in front of them. The energy licked the stones that contained the event horizon. Kyle stood in amazement at the portal, an image of another place inside. Kyle stood to the side of the stone to see that the image within the portal did not change.

"What is this?" He asked.

"Where we need to go, step through before it closes." Kyle began to take his steps towards the portal, but his conscience held him in place. Looking back at a defenceless Domina, he knew he couldn't leave her, even if he couldn't trust her.

"We need to take her." Kyle expressed. Ezekiel came to a stop just before the portal.

"We can't take her, she's not to be trusted." Kyle still knew in his heart leaving her would be killing her.

"I can't go knowing we left her to die." Kyle now pleaded.

"We need to take her."

"Nzara-Fűn" Ezekiel growled as he stormed over to Domina and threw her over his shoulder with one hand. He walked effortlessly carrying her to the portal. "I have her, now go through before I kick you through."

Kyle didn't wait to find out if the threat was a bluff as he stepped through.

Every inch of his body tingled as he emerged on the other side. The jump seemed to be instantaneous as he looked back to see the snowy ruins he had just stood in. A moment later Ezekiel stepped through and the portal began to evaporate into thin air.

"Be careful, the first time people go through are always sick."

"I feel fine." Kyle replied. The tingling quickly changed as his stomach wrenched causing him to vomit immediately. Ezekiel chuckled as Kyle continued to up the contents of his stomach.

"It never gets old. Better smarten yourself up, we will be meeting them soon."

"Meeting who?" Kyle grumbled as he spat out the remnants from his mouth.

"The council is this way, we're already expected."

Kyle looked around them expecting to see something remarkable. Instead he was greeted with an ice cave, the floor was wet bare rock as dark as the Dwarf's eyes. The two trudged down a path that looked to have been carved into the very rock. Every now and then Kyle slipped on the water that ran over the ground. He was surprised by the cave. 'I thought it'd be colder' Kyle thought as he looked at the ice above, instead it was surprisingly warm. A breeze blew through the cave carrying a vague but inviting smell in the air.

"Is this your city?" Kyle wondered. Ezekiel shook his head.

"No, it's yours." He responded. Kyle was baffled by his answer. 'Surely we're not at Rheia' He thought, 'there are no caves.'

His train of thought was interrupted by the vista before him. The confined ice cave opened up into a monstrous domed cavern. The ice shelf above them had moulded over a huge sprawling city. Each section of the city had a tower that dominated its district and at its centre a road leading to a light. The images on the wall at the ruins did nothing to capture the majesty of the city now standing in front of him. Light from the centre reflected softly down onto the city and cavern below. Kyle's mouth was ajar as he stared in silence at the metropolis.

"Come, the council is waiting for us."

They both continued their descent until finally reaching the cavern floor.

Kyle continued to be memorized by the sight of the city. He could scarcely believe that he might be looking upon the city of light, the birthplace of the heroes of the world. Cyrilla.

A head of them was a door that befitted a city of such a size. Already standing open with a group of people waiting patiently at the threshold to the city, Kyle studied each one of them as he approached, each dressed in a distinct colour trimmed with golds, silvers and jade. A couple were clad in a reflective armour Kyle had never seen before. One man and woman stood out the most to him. The woman had a rosy complexion to her cheeks, her dress embroidered with ornate leather strips. Her hair was tied back and laced with golden ribbons. The man stood tall and proud, his back straight, his shoulders wide. His clothing was less militaristic as he wore silks and fur. Ezekiel came to a stop a few metres away and bowed lightly still holding Domina over his shoulder. Kyle bowed as well.

"Greetings Ezekiel, friend of Cyrilla. These are indeed strange gifts you bring us from your people."

"They're not gifts lord, instead I bring you Duŕum, Nightsbane."

The people muttered to themselves before the Lord turned his attention to Kyle.

"What is your name, master?"

"Kyle" He stuttered nervously, "I'm Kyle of Rheia"

"Well Kyle of Rheia, I am Haza'Zem Ori, I am the leader of this council."

Each one of the councillors politely bowed their heads towards Kyle before standing firm again. Their greeting was very formal which made him nervous about doing something wrong. Haza took a step forward towards Kyle. "Tell me, how do you know he is a Nightsbane master Dwarf?"

"I witnessed him carrying the amulet of Bellatris and I have seen him display powers I have not seen in all my years." Ezekiel claimed, "He is the one, I'm sure of it."

Kyle's nerves grew as they began to talk about him in front of him. Each one of the councillors inspected and judged him.

"My Lord, Ezekiel is wrong, I did have the amulet, but it was taken from me by someone very powerful." Kyle said, "I fear he is going to unleash Nightshade on the world, you have to do something."

The council stared at him, a feeling of judgement weighed heavy on him.

"This is very grave news indeed; we will summon a council meeting immediately." Haza replied rather calmly. Kyle was astounded by his reaction to the news. Impending doom was almost certain, and they reacted as if a leaf had fallen. Kyle was not used to the attention being placed on him and in instinct he placed his hand on his sword. Haza saw the slight movement.

"There is no need to touch that here, no harm shall come to you as you are our guest." Haza eyed up the sword. "That is an interesting blade you carry, may Lady Izella inspect it?"

The rosy woman stepped forward and walked up to Kyle. He politely nodded and unsheathed his sword. Izella held the sword out and began to swing the sword with a beautiful grace, light bounced off the edge of the blade as it sliced through the air. Satisfied she handed the sword back to him.

"Beautiful blade, I've not seen a blade as fine as this for many centuries." She remarked as she fell back to her original position.

"Centuries? Forgive me Lady but you look as young as me. Surely you meant years?"

Izella opened her mouth ready to speak but Haza held his hand up.

"I believe you have many questions on your mind master Kyle." He smiled, "and all will be answered in good time but for now let me welcome you to Cyrilla."

Haza extended his arm towards the gates and the city beyond. Hesitation came over him as he looked on at the city he had imagined for so long. The books he read telling tales of old and the deeds of the city and now standing in front of it, Kyle felt overwhelmed. He looked to Ezekiel and Domina who still laid unconscious on his shoulder. His mind wandered to the meeting of Idella on the mountain top. Her words rang out in his head. 'You will not be alone.' Kyle felt as if his journey had only just begun as he took his first step towards the city.

A Nightmare Unleashed
Chapter 25

The sound of birds and insects had disappeared from their surroundings as Keela, Ariel and the other Blades made their way deeper into the forest. With each mile the air became close and windless, the trees neither waved in the breeze nor creaked, just silent as stone. As they closed in towards the mountain the trees became denser, their roots thicker and entwined as if they were one. Ariel thought the forest was sick or cursed, feeling a weight of darkness on her shoulders. She could see the other blades felt the same as they trekked through the dense forest. Keela on the other hand moved forward without so much of a struggle as he clambered through, his mind fixed on the coming event.

Everyone knew about the final battle of the Dawning war, it was taught to children at a young age, scholars still debate the history of the events of that time, even she remembered her teacher reading about it to her. The words always made the battles seem trivial but now standing in the forest, seeing how confining the fight would have been, she thought about the dead that lay hewn on the ground. Every crack under her boots made her wonder what was cracking, branches or bone. Standing high above the trees the reason for their being, the final destination, Telloma. Standing anywhere in West Laxos the mountain could be seen but at its base, the mountain engulfed the sky. Trees ran up its base before giving way to rocks and eventually snow. No one had ever climbed to the summit and lived, thankfully Ariel thought their journey was nearing the end as a large cave appeared through the trees. A break in the trees allowed them all to see the maw in front of them. A crack as tall as any building in any city, it could easily have been mistaken for a god hitting the mountain. Tree stumps and desiccated trunks lay scattered and splintered about the entrance, the last remaining evidence of a battle long ago, others had been cut down and stacked in a pile many years ago, a reminder of their devotion to their task.

"We're here, can you feel it?" Keela rejoiced. "The power of this place fills the air."

He wasn't wrong, Ariel could feel something on her skin, a tingle of energy that made the hairs on her arms and neck stand up. It felt wrong to her, never had she been to a place that felt so corrupt. Some of the Blades began to show a little apprehension about going into the cave. With the sun beating down on them, the entrance beyond the threshold seemed to deflect any light leaving it in darkness. Keela smiled as he looked back at Ariel who looked concerned.

"It's our time." He spoke.

Ariel loved him but feared what may happen inside the cave. Showing her devotion, Ariel forced a smile and nodded. Keela without hesitation marched into the maw. Ariel glanced over to the other Blades who looked to her for courage. She took a deep breath and walked towards the cave. The sensation on her skin grew the closer she came to the threshold.

Deeper inside, the darkness was darker than any night she had witnessed, the smell of damp filled the air. Ahead a small light glowed from the void. Suddenly a burst of flame came into being causing Ariel to look behind her. A couple of Blades had fashioned a torch out of broken branches and anything they could use to create light. The group continued deeper into the cave, all along the wall scratches and gashes were taken out of the rock. Deep grooves looked as if weapons had slashed through the granite rock. Ariel imagined the fight between Arturus, Bellatris and Nightshade, the power all three wielded and the destruction they created.

Keela had told her the Dawning war was needed to purge the arrogance of man. He spoke of Cyrillia and its people defying the gods and expanding beyond what they could comprehend. Cirdire was the pinnacle of their arrogance until Shassa blessed him with a purpose. Transforming him into Nightshade, he now had the responsibility of correcting the balance of the world. Millenia later, Keela believed he was responsible for carrying on the mantle. "Brothers, Sisters we are here." Keela shouted, his voice echoing around them. They came to a stop behind Keela. before them the path opened out into a cavern of magnificent proportions. The cavern must have been the heart of the mountain, it's walls rose high into the darkness and similarly fell in an abyss. At the centre a plateau that extended into the middle. A single large rock stood in the centre.
Ariel felt uneasy about everything. Monks, soldiers, anyone associated with the relics they had collected had fought hard to keep them safe and it was as easy walking into the cave. 'Not a single trap or spell' she thought as she walked forward. Her eyes scanned the walls and floor hoping to find an ancient trap, something to put her mind at ease. Nothing. They all continued to walk to the plateau in the middle, the path became harder to see as they reached the middle, surrounding them in darkness. One step either side and they would fall into the void below. Ariel wondered how far it fell, the urge to know became a

question to distract her from the unease in her mind.

Keela walked up to the rock and held his hand out. For a moment he held it just away from the surface expecting something to attack him.

Nothing but silence.

His excitement was too much for fear to hold him back. The power he could wield was only fingertips away, his time to rule within his grasp. The rock was littered with runes and carvings that only a few could read. One passage that Keela could easily cypher read:

"Here lies the Betrayer, the Faithless, Nightshade. Bound and shackled to this realm and entombed in the earth. He shall remain in darkness, never to be released upon the world. His body will fade but his essence shall never rest..."

Keela traced his hands over the words, a bitterness in his heart as he continued to read the final inscription.

"...Any who release him shall become him, bound and cursed"

Keela turned to his followers and opened a pouch on his side. Inside he pulled out Seven stones and passed them to each one.

"Quickly brothers, our destiny is here." Keela snapped as he directed them to stand around the rock. On the ground looked to be small dips as if something had crushed the ground. As each one of the Blades came to a spot and their stone glowed a strange hue. Ariel watched as each one took their place. She turned to Keela.

"What happens now?" Ariel asked. Without a word, he smiled before turning back to the rock. Keela pulled the amulet from his pocket and stepped towards a groove in the rock. Keela slowly placed his hand into the recess of the rock all the way up to his elbow and felt the amulet Slide into place.

A loud crunch sounded.

Locked and holding Keela's hand in place he looked to his followers who themselves now looked confused and frightened. The stones in their hands beamed brightly towards the rock. Some tried to move but were locked in place as Keela was, the light intensifying. Ariel stepped forward to Keela

"No, do not come any closer my love, it will be alright."

Keela snapped, "It is a test."

Keela screamed as the lock clamped harder and pulled his arm in. The light from the stones permeated the ground and rand towards the rock and up its surface. The mixture of colours and screams was both beautiful and terrifying to behold as Ariel was helpless. Each one of the followers screamed in agony as they were consumed by the light. After a few seconds all fell silent as the rock face cracked and crumbled to the ground. Keela dropped to his knees in exhaustion clutching his arm, all the clothing and flesh had been stripped away. The followers who had held the stones now lay dead, drained of life and turned to husks. The dust settled around them to reveal inside the rock was a tomb, a mummified body bound in irons. On its face was a look of anguish. Keela looked at the face in front of him, the face of his master Nightshade. On its neck was a brand that had been burnt into his skin. Betrayer.

A shriek echoed out of the darkness, but Keela could not take his eyes off the face. With a violent force a black phantom poured out of the mummy and forced itself into every opening in Keela. His scream masked by the shrill of the phantom. A moment passed, and all fell to silence once more. Keela felt his mind cloud as he stood to his feet, power raced through his body. He turned to Ariel who was shocked and concerned at everything she witnessed.

"It's ok, it is over." Keela said calmly. He inspected his body as he continued to feel something powerful inside. "You cannot imagine the power I now hold."

Within seconds the flesh that had been stripped from his arm rapidly grew back, all the scars had disappeared too. Ariel looked at the bodies of her brothers and sisters, followers who now laid dead.

"What about them, they're all dead." Ariel asked. "They trusted you?"

"And now they shall bask in my power." Keela confidently spoke, raising his arms. As they raised higher, each one of the corpses twitched and moved. They began to stumble and stagger to their feet, the macabre dance of still withered husks. Their clothes had turned to rags from the power of the stones which Ariel could see had fused into their hands.

"As you can see, they are now eternal, like you." Keela added. Power pulsed through his veins as he looked at her. His smile faded as he felt something within pierced his heart.

Keela felt a pain he'd never felt. Falling to his knees, Keela screamed as his skin turned to ash as it cracked and peeled away. Ariel dropped to her knees next to him helpless once more as she watched Keela writhe in agony. The phantom appeared next to her.

"Now I am reborn." It whispered. Keela looked at the phantom who smiled back at him. "A willing pawn you have been, now I shall finish what was started many ages ago."

Keela let out a final scream as the power within him warped his body and mind. He felt his essence of his being become chained and encased in his own mind as the phantom imprisoned him. A burst of energy pushed Ariel away. The force was so hard she nearly fell off the edge of the plateau. Clawing desperately to climb back over the edge she reached for a protruding stone and grabbed it. With a heave she pulled herself up and rolled onto her back breathing deeply.

Now standing where Keela was, someone who resembled him but twisted and unnatural form. His skin was the colour of ash, his eyes red as flame and his veins glowed red as well. His brown hair had turned black as the clothes he wore. His hands now stretched resembled claws long and pointed. All the Blades stood emotionless behind him awaiting a command.

Nightshade had been reborn.

Glancing over at Ariel with intent and extending its hand out towards her. Shocked at what her Keela had become, she on instinct met his grasp and was pulled up. Gazing into his eyes she could see fire raging in his soul as if hell was only an inch away.

"Come child." Nightshade commanded, its voice broken and scratched but still commanding. As frightened as she was, she complied. It had been a long time since she had felt any resemblance of fear and now, she walked among it.

The silent march out of the cave was met with blinding light. Her eyes struggled to adjust to it for a moment, but Nightshade and his new Blades felt nothing. Nightshade scanned the terrain ahead, memories flooded back as if the battle was yesterday. His followers and enemies fought fiercely he thought 'and so they shall again.' Keela raised his hand as Mana warped around his body. With an almighty thud he forced his fist into the ground. The Mana ripped through the ground all around them as cracks opened up.

"Rise my fallen champions." Nightshade bellowed. "You have slept for too long and now it is time to take back what was taken from you."

Arms, legs and heads burst through the dirt. Skulls and decayed bodies clambered to their feet followed by demonic beings. Ariel watched on as an army of dead, ancient soldiers rose still clad in their armour.

Nightshade's mouth cracked as he smiled. Pieces of skin fell away from the edges to reveal the teeth and tendon beneath.

"This is just the beginning." He turned to Ariel. Nightshade stepped forward to address the dead.

"Too long you have slept as the world around has grown corrupt, hateful and divided." He shouted. "Now it is time for me to rule." He said to himself. Unsheathing his sword, it caught fire as its blue flames lashed off the blade. An awful shriek came from Nightshade as he screamed, pointing his sword forward. In unison the army turned and slowly marched into the forest, their bones creaking under the weight of their armour and weapons. The Dawning war was over, but right now a new war was descended upon the world.

End

MAP OF
LAXOS WEST

THE GREAT OCEAN

THE SOMERIAN SEA

SHANKTOWN

NORTHERN WASTES

IRRAGIN

AERILON

ARTHERIA

DAIRY

RHEIA

AULT

NAPORIA

DOVEPORT

CLOWETTA

AYNOR

KELD

TELLOMA

BELTORIA

TYKE

PENKETH
KEEP

ASTRAK
KEEP

TAKERS
KEEP

WOLFDEN
KEEP

CYRILLA

EASTBOUNRE

Note from the author

Thank you so much for reading Mana Borne *'Amulet of Heroes'*. I hope you enjoyed it! It would mean a lot if you would be kind enough to leave a review on Amazon.

Book reviews help readers find and discover indie authors like me to find new fans. It will also help me to know how I might improve on the next books.

The second book of the Mana Borne series, Rise of Nightshade, is due to be published around Christmas 2021.

If you would like to find out more or want to jump into the world of Mana Borne follow my page on Facebook Mana Borne Book Series, for more info, special offers and so much more.

There are also the short stories which tie into the main books. Each one follows a character and explores a little of their back story.

This book was written by someone with Dyslexia and proofread however there may be some errors, please bare this in mind. It is meant to inspire people who struggle to read or write.

Thank you again.